Travesty

by john hawkes

Charivari (in *Lunar Landscapes*)

The Cannibal

The Beetle Leg

The Goose on the Grave & The Owl

The Owl

The Lime Twig

Second Skin

The Innocent Party (plays)

Lunar Landscapes (stories & short novels)

The Blood Oranges

Death, Sleep & the Traveler

Travesty

Virginie: Her Two Lives

The Passion Artist

Humors of Blood & Skin: A John Hawkes Reader

I am imbued with the notion that a Muse is necessarily a dead woman, inaccesible or absent; that the poetic structure—like the canon, which is only a hole surrounded by steel—can be based only on what one does not have; and that ultimately one can write only to fill a void or at the least to situate, in relation to the most lucid part of ourselves, the place where this incommensurable abyss yawns within us.

—*Michel Leiris:* Manhood

You see, a person I knew used to divide human beings into three categories: those who prefer having nothing to hide rather than being obliged to lie, those who prefer lying to having nothing to hide, and finally those who like both lying and the hidden. I'll let you choose the pigeonhole that suits me.

—*Albert Camus:* The Fall

john hawkes

Travesty

A *New Directions* Book

Portions of this book first appeared in *Fiction* and *Tri-Quarterly*,
to whose editors grateful acknowledgment is made.

The epigraphic passages to this work are quoted from Michel Leiris'
Manhood: A Journey from Childhood into the Fierce Order of Virility
(Copyright © 1963 by Grossman Publishers), translated by Richard Howard
and published by Grossman Publishers, and Albert Camus' *The Fall*
(Copyright © 1956 by Alfred A. Knopf, Inc.), translated by Justin O'Brien
and published by Random House, Inc.

Manufactured in the United States of America
New Directions books are printed on acid-free paper.
First published clothbound by New Directions in 1976
and as New Directions Paperbook 430 in 1977.
Published simultaneously in Canada by Penguin Books Canada Limited

Library of Congress Cataloging in Publication Data

Hawkes, John, 1925–
Travesty.

(A New Directions Book)
I. Title.
PZ3.H3132Tr   [PS3558.A82]   813'.5'4   75-26764
ISBN 0-8112-0597-5
ISBN 0-8112-0640-8 pbk.

Designed by Gertrude Huston

New Directions Books are published for James Laughlin
by New Directions Publishing Corporation,
80 Eighth Avenue, New York 10011

FIFTH PRINTING

For Three Sophies

Travesty

No, no, Henri. Hands off the wheel. Please. It is too late. After all, at one hundred and forty-nine kilometers per hour on a country road in the darkest quarter of the night, surely it is obvious that your slightest effort to wrench away the wheel will pitch us into the toneless world of highway tragedy even more quickly than I have planned. And you will not believe it, but we are still accelerating.

As for you, Chantal, you must beware. You must obey your Papa. You must sit back in your seat and fasten your belt and stop crying. And Chantal, no more beating the driver about the shoulders or shaking his arm. Emulate Henri, my poor Chantal, and control yourself.

11

travesty

But see how we fly! And the curves, how sharp and numerous they are! The geometrics of joy!

At least you are in the hands of an expert driver.

So you are going to relax, *cher ami*. You are determined to hide your trembling, achieve a few moments of silence, begin smoking one of your delightful cigarettes, and then after this appropriate expenditure of precious time and in the midst of your composure, then you will attempt to dissuade me, to talk me back to sanity (as you will express the idea), to appeal to my kindness and good sense. I approve. I am listening. The hour is yours. But of course you may use the lighter. Only reach for it slowly and keep in mind my warning. Do not be deceived by my good nature. I am as serious as a sheet of flame.

As for you, Chantal, you must stop that sobbing. I will not say it again. Don't you know that Papa loves you? Not many young women have the opportunity of passing their last minutes in the company of lover and loving Papa both. The black night, the speeding car, the three of us, a glimpse of early snow curled in the roots of a fleeting roadside tree—it is a warm and comfortable way to go, Chantal. You must not be afraid.

And to think that we used to call her the "porno brat." Yes, our own Chantal—no sooner was she able to walk than she was forever stumbling into the erotic lives of her parents. Or perhaps I should say the illusory lives of her young parents. At any rate it was Honorine who began to call our own baby girl the "porno brat." But with a smile. Always with that ingenuous smile so appropriate to the oval and sensual face of the woman who is your mistress, my wife, Chantal's still young and generous mother. And then there was the schoolmate of Chantal's, that boyish jokester, who gave her the optician's chart with its letters diminishing in size and saying TOO MUCH SEX MAKES ONE SHORTSIGHTED.

But do you know that I have never worn eyeglasses and even now am permitted to drive the fastest cars without anything at all to assist the sight of my naked eyes?

But Chantal and Honorine—what a pair of names. And to think that at this instant the one is white-faced, tear-streaked and clinging to the edge of hysteria in lieu of prayer directly behind us, while the other sleeps in the very chateau we are approaching. But be brave, Chantal. There will be no comforting Honorine when she receives the news.

Murder, Henri? Well, that is precisely the trouble with you poets. In your pessimism you ape the articulation you achieve in written words, you are able to recite your poems as an actor his lines, you consider yourselves quite exempt from all those rules of behavior that constrict us lesser-privileged men in feet, hands, loins, mouths. Yet in the last extremity you cry moral wolf. So you accuse me of planning murder. But with the very use of the word you reveal at last that you are only the most banal and predictable of poets. No libertine, no man of vision and hence suffering, but a banal moralist. Think of the connotations of "murder," that awful word: the loss of emotional control, the hate, the spite, the selfishness, the broken glass, the blood, the cry in the throat, the trembling blindness that results in the irrevocable act, the helpless blow. Murder is the most limited of gestures.

But how different is our own situation. Suspended as you are in time, holding your lighted cigarette between your fingers, bathed in your own sweat and the gentle lights of the dashboard—in all this there is clarity but not morality. Not even ethics. You and Chantal and I are simply traveling in purity and extremity down that road the rest of the world attempts to hide from us by heaping up whole forests of the most confusing road signs, detours, barricades. What does it matter that the choice is mine, not yours? That I am the driver and you the passenger? Can't you see that your morality is no different from Chantal's whimpering and that here, now, we are dealing with a question of choice rather than chaos?

I am no poet. And I am no murderer. But did Chantal ever tell you about the time she won for herself the

14

travesty

title "Queen of Carrots?" No? But perhaps your sexual knowledge of my daughter has made you shortsighted after all.

I am not laughing at you. I am the kindest man you will ever meet.

Slow down, you say? But the course of events cannot be regulated by some sort of perversely wired traffic policeman. We do not argue with the star, the comet, the locomotive racing almost invisible in the cold night, the conductor on the empty but moving *autobus*. I am not a child. I trust you not to demean yourself with mere transparency or pathos. Our speed is a maximum in a bed of maximums which happen to include: my driving skill, this empty road, the time of night, the capacity of the car's engine, the immensity of the four seasons lying beyond us between the trees or in the flat fields. Like schoolboys who have studied the solar system (I do not mean to be condescending or simple-minded) you and I know that all the elements of life coerce each other, force each other instant by instant into that perfect formation which is lofty and the only one possible. I am aware of a particular distance; these yellow headlights are the lights of my eyes; my mind is bound inside my memory of this curving road like a fist in glass.

You cannot know how often I have driven this

travesty

precise route alone and at the fastest speed I could achieve. You cannot be aware of those innumerable late afternoons each of which contained this silent car, the technician sprawled on his back beneath my car, a bank of chromium instruments, a silence only faintly smelling of grease and oil, myself as the patient spectator in one corner of a place that resembled the nearly empty interior of an aircraft hangar. There, there is your speed. Would you believe it?

Between the adjustments made by the hand of that white-coated figure lying as if dead on the concrete floor of his vast garage, and the warm and living pressure of my own two hands on the thick black skin of this steering wheel—from that time to this, from one hand to a pair of hands, from the minute adjustments made beneath the car to the life of the mind that holds the moving car to the road, there is nothing, nothing at all.

The last time I drove this car to that garage I shook hands with the technician. On the ramp the waiting automobile gleamed as new. Now we are traveling as if inside a clock the shape of a bullet, seated as if stationary among tight springs and brilliant gems. And we have a full tank of fuel, and tires hardly a month old.

Do not ask me to slow down. It is impossible.

But you are already loosening your collar while I ramble on about Chantal's childhood, my love of cars,

travesty

the intimacy we share, our swift progress through the fortress of space. Suddenly you and I are more different than ever, yet closer even than when we were three to a bed. But don't worry, despite all this talk of mine I am concentrating. Never for an instant do I lose sight of the road we follow through our blackest night, though I can hardly see it. Yes, my concentration is like that of a marksman, a tasteful executioner, a child crouching over a bug on a stick. And I understand your frustration, your feelings of incomprehension. It is not easy to discover that your closest friend and husband to one mistress and father of the other is driving at something greater than his customary speed, at a speed that begins to frighten you, and that this same friend is driving by plan, intentionally, and refuses to listen to what for you is reason. What can you do? How in but a few minutes can you adjust yourself successfully to what for me is second nature: a nearly phobic yearning for the truest paradox, a thirst to lie at the center of this paradigm: one moment the car in perfect condition, without so much as a scratch on its curving surface, the next moment impact, sheer impact. Total destruction. In its own way it is a form of ecstasy, this utter harmony between design and debris. But even a poet will find it difficult to share this vision on short notice.

But Chantal, perhaps you would like to remove your shoes. Perhaps you would like to imagine that you are merely one of several hundred airplane passengers preparing themselves to survive if possible a crash landing. And yet we are only three. Only three. A small but soothing number.

Of course I am not joking. How for the briefest pleasure of joking could I risk the lives of my own daughter and a poet acclaimed by the public? I am certainly not the man to take risks or live or for that matter die by chance. I am disappointed. Apparently your need to be spared—your need for relief, for deceleration—is so great that now, after all these years, you are willing to do even the most terrible injustice to my character, merely for the sake of your urgency. You wish only to open your eyes and find us safely parked on the edge of the dark road, the interior of the automobile filled with our soft and private laughter. I understand. But I regret that it cannot be that way, *cher ami.*

Why not alone? Or why not the four of us? Well, these are much more serious and interesting questions. At last you perceive that I am not merely some sort of suicidal maniac, an aesthetician of death at high speed. But even to approach these subtle thoughts you must give me time, more time. And yet doesn't the fact that you've asked the first question hint at least at its answer?

Please, I beg you. Do not accuse me of being a man without feeling or a man of unnatural feeling. This moment, for instance, is not disgusting but decisive. The reason I am feeling a sensation of comfort so intense as to be almost electrical, while you on the other hand are feeling only a mixture of disbelief and misery—the reason for this disparity between us is more, much more, than a matter of temperament, though it is that too. We have agreed on the surface aspects of trauma: the difficulty of submission, the problem of surprise, a concept of existence so suddenly constricted that one feels like a goldfish crazed and yet at the same time quite paralyzed in his bowl. A mere question of adjustment. But the fact of the matter is that you do not share my interest in what I have called "design and debris." For instance, you and I are equally familiar with our white avenues, our sunlit thoroughfares, our boulevards beautifully packed with vehicles which even at a standstill are able to careen about. The bright colors, the shouts, the bestial roar of the traffic, the policemen typically wired for contradictory signals—it is a commonplace, not worth a thought. And you and I are equally familiar with those occasional large patches of sand which fill half the street, marking the site of one of our frequent and incomprehensible collisions, and around which the traffic is forced impatiently to veer—until some courageous driver falls back on good sense and lunges straight across the patch of sand, his tires scattering the sand and revealing the fresh blood beneath. Another commonplace, you say, more everyday life. The triteness of a nation incapable of understanding highway, motor vehicle, pedestrian.

travesty

But here we differ, because I have always been secretly drawn to the scene of accidents, have always paused beside those patches of sand with a certain quickening of pulse and hardening of concentration. Mere sand, mere sand flung down on a city street and already sponging up the blood beneath. But for me these small islands created out of haste, pain, death, crudeness, are thoroughly analogous to the symmetry of the two or even more machines whose crashing results in nothing more than an aftermath of blood and sand. It is like a skin, this small area of dusty butchery, that might have been peeled from the body of one of the offending cars. I think of the shot tiger and the skin in the hall of the dark chateau. But for you it is worth no more than a shrug. Your poetry lies elsewhere. Whereas I have never failed to pull over, park, alight from my automobile—despite the honking, the insults—and spend my few moments of reverential amazement whenever and wherever I have discovered one of these sacred sites. It is something like a war memorial. The greater the incongruity, the greater the truth.

But what about me, you are asking yourself, what about my life? My safety? And why am I now subjected to foolish philosophy mouthed by a man who has suddenly become an insufferable egotist and who threatens to kill me, maim me, by smashing this car into the trunk of an unmoving tree in ten minutes, or twenty, or thirty?

Now you must listen. The point is that you cannot imagine that I, the head of the household, so to speak, can behave in this fashion; you cannot believe that a life as rich as yours, as sensual as yours, as honored, can suddenly be reduced inexplicably to fear, grief, skid marks, a few shards of broken glass; you simply do not know that as a child I divided my furtive time quite equally between those periodicals depicting the most brutal and uncanny destructions of human flesh (the elbow locked inside the mouth, the head half buried inside the chest, the statuary of severed legs, dangling hands) and those other periodicals depicting the attractions of young living women partially or totally in the nude.

Spare me, you cry. Spare me. But the lack of knowledge and lack of imagination are yours, not mine. And it will not be against a tree. There you are even more grossly mistaken.

Remind me to tell you about little Pascal. He was Chantal's little brother and died around the time Honorine nicknamed Chantal the "porno brat." My son, my own son, who died just at the moment of acquiring character. Even now the white satin hangs in shreds from the arms of the stone cross that marks his grave.

Very well. No radio. Music, no music, it is all the same to me, though had the thought been agreeable to

travesty

you, I suppose I might have preferred the gentlest background of some score prepared for melodrama. No doubt I am attracted to the sentimentality of flute, drum, orchestra, simply because listening to music is exactly like hurtling through the night in a warm car: the musical experience, like the automobile, guarantees timelessness, or so it appears. The song and road are endless, or so we think. And yet they are not. The beauty of motion, musical or otherwise, is precisely this: that the so-called guarantee of timelessness is in fact the living tongue in the dark mouth of cessation. And cessation is what we seek, if only because it alone is utterly unbelievable.

But Chantal is not listening. She is preoccupied with an agony even greater than yours. She cannot care that recently her Papa has begun to think about our several lives. But of course from you I expect total attention. We are grown men, after all, and have eaten from the same bowl often enough. As for me, in this instance I respect your wishes. My beautiful high-fidelity radio stays dead.

Let us hope that I have not miscalculated and that there is not some overblown machine now lumbering down upon us, filling the road ahead, its great belly brimming with thick liquid fire and, in its noisy cab, a gargantuan young peasant singing to keep himself awake. Disaster. Witless, idiotic disaster. Because what I have in mind is an "accident" so perfectly contrived that it will be unique, spectacular, instantaneous, a physical counterpart to that vision in which it was in fact conceived. A clear "accident," so to speak, in which invention quite defies interpretation.

In the first place I fully intend us to pass the dark chateau where our own Honorine lies sleeping. We will be traveling at our highest speed, of course, and already will have reached the top of our arc. But perhaps for an instant our lights will somehow intrude upon Honorine's interior life, or perhaps even the sound of our passing—that faint horrifying expulsion of breath which is the combination of tires and engine racing together at a great distance—may somehow attract the briefest response from Honorine's dormant consciousness. She will move an arm, make a sound, roll over, who knows? Then eight kilometers beyond the chateau and we approach the old Roman viaduct. You remember it, that narrow dead viaduct that spans the dry gorge and always reminds me of flaking bone. Of course you remember it. And in the smallest imaginable amount of time our demon steel shall fuse its speed with the stasis of old stone. The sides of our handsome car shall nearly touch the low balustrades of that high and rarely traversed construction, we shall all three of us be aware of the roar of stone, the sound of space, our headlights boring across the gorge as in a cheap film. And now, now you are thinking that here is the spot where it shall

all end. Yes, here would be the natural site of what will be called our "tragic accident." Roman time, modern car, insufficient space between the balustrades, the appalling distance to the rocks in the bottom of the gorge, the uneven surface of the roadway across that viaduct. . . . What could be better? But you are wrong.

Because that is the problem. Precisely. All those "logical" details and all those lofty "symbols" of melodrama speak much too clearly to the professional investigator (and reporter) of such events. No, we shall not be able to crash off the viaduct or even miss it altogether and so sail directly into the wilderness of that deep gorge like some stricken winged demon from the books of childhood. Instead we shall merely continue beyond the viaduct about three kilometers (hardly the twitch of a lid, the snap of a head) where we shall make an impossible turn onto the premises of an abandoned farm and there, with no slackening of pace, run squarely into the windowless wall of an old and now roofless barn built lovingly, long ago, of great stones from the field. That wall is a meter thick. A full meter, or even slightly more.

The car that passes the very chateau that must have been its destination; the unmistakable tire tracks across the viaduct; the turn that is nothing less than incomprehensible; the tremendous speed upon impact; the failure of the autopsy to reveal the slightest trace of alcohol in the corpse of the driver. . . . What can they think? What can they possibly produce as explanation? What will they say about an event as severe and improbable as this one will appear to be, as well as one loud enough to wake the curate in the little nearby village of La Roche?

But that is exactly the point, since what is happening now must be senseless to everyone except possibly the occupants of the demolished car. During the—let me see—next hour and forty minutes by the dashboard clock, it will be up to the three of us to make what we can of this experience. And we will not be able to count on Chantal for any very meaningful contribution.

At any rate the lumbering disruptive oil truck is out of the question. Out of the question. Nothing will destroy the symmetry I have in mind. Don't you agree?

I have never seen the old curate of La Roche, but I know that he coughs a great deal and has a tobacco breath and that his fingers are forever stained with wine. But he is a deep and noisy sleeper, of that I am certain. What an irony that the co-ordinates of space and time have fixed on him to be our Chanticleer, so to speak, and that it will be he who will offer the first cockcrow to the explosion that will inaugurate our silence. Which reminds me, only yesterday I sat in this very automobile and watched an old couple helping each other down a village street (not La Roche, I have never been in La Roche) toward a life-sized and freshly painted wooden Christ-on-the-Cross mounted on a stone block not far from where I sat in my car. The old man, who was holding the woman's elbow, was a thin and obviously bad-tempered captive of marriage. The old woman was bow-legged. Or at least her short legs angled out from where her knees must have been beneath the heavy skirts, and then jutted together sharply at the ankles. This creature depended for locomotion on the lifetime partner inching along at her side. The old man was wearing a white sporting cap and carrying the woman's new leather sack. The old woman, heavily bandaged about the throat in an atrocious violet muffler, was carrying a little freshly picked bouquet of flowers. Well, it's a simple story. This scowling pair progressed beyond my silent automobile (you must imagine the incongruity of the old married couple, the orange roof tiles, the waiting Christ, the beige-colored lacquer of this automobile gleaming impressively in the bright sunlight) until at last the woman deposited the trim little bouquet of flowers at the feet of the Christ.

There you have it. Ours is a country of coughers and worshipers. Between the two I choose the coughers. At least there is something especially attractive about one of our schoolyards of coughing children, don't you agree? The incipient infection is livelier than the health it destroys. Yes, I do appreciate that hacking music and all their little faces so bright and blighted.

But have I never told you I am missing a lung? The war of course. That is another story. Perhaps we shall get to it. At any rate it is probably true that my missing lung determined long ago my choice of a doctor. You see, my poor doctor is missing one leg (the left,

travesty

I believe) which was amputated only weeks before the
poor fellow's wife ran off, finally, with her lover of about
twenty years' standing. It was a compounded shock, an
unusual circumstance, and as soon as I learned of it I
became an additional patient on the diminishing roster
of my crippled physician. The affinity is obvious, obvious. But by now you will have perceived the design
that underlies all my rambling and which, like a giant
snow crystal, permeates all the tissues of existence. But
the crystal melts, the tissues dissolve, a doctor's leg is
neatly amputated by a team of doctors. Design and
debris, as I have said already. Design and debris. I thrive
on it. For me the artificial limb is more real, if you will
allow the word, than the other and natural limb still in-
habited by sensation. But I know you, *cher ami.* You
are interested not in the doctor's amputated leg but in
his missing wife. Well, each man to his taste. At least
I can report that my physician is highly skilled, despite
all his cigarettes and his trembling hands. Incidentally,
his cough is one of the worst I have ever heard.

But you are groaning. And yet even now we have
so far to go that I cannot help but advise you to con-
serve the sounds in your throat. That's better, much
better. But must you wring your hands? Remember, you
are setting a firm example for Chantal.

Yes, it seems to me that one of the strongest grati-
fications of night driving is precisely that you can see so
little, and yet at the same time see so very much. The

travesty

child awakes in us once again when we drive at night, and then all those earliest sensations of fear and security begin shimmering, tingling once again inside ourselves. The car is dark, we hear lost voices, the dials glow, and simultaneously we are moving and not moving, held deep in the comfort of the cushions as once we were on just such a night as this one, yet feeling even in the softness of the beige upholstery all the sickening texture of our actual travel. As children we had absolute confidence in the driver, although there was always the delicious possibility of a wrong turn, some mechanical failure, all the distant unknowns of the night itself. And then there was sight, whatever we could see to the sides of the car or on the road ahead, and it was all so utterly dependent on the headlights, and sight so uncontrollably reduced was of course all the more magnified and pleasing.

It is no different now. Even setting aside our projected destination, which to me is the final blinding piece in a familiar puzzle, the fourth and solid wall in a room of glass, the clear burst of desire that is never entirely out of my mind, while for you it is quite the opposite, since what you know about our particular journey blunts you to the pleasures of this road, this night, this conversation, so that you and I are like two dancers at arm's length, regurgitation locked together with ingestion in a formal, musical embrace. . . . But setting all this aside, as I say, there is still the undeniable world of our night driving, and it is alluring, prohibitive, personal, a mystery that is in fact quite specific, since it is common to child, to lovers, to the lone man driving from one dark town to the next.

Yes, raise your eyes. Look through the clear glass of the windshield while it is still intact. There, do you see how the outer edges of the cone of light shudder against the flanks of darkness? And look at the actual length of our yellow beams, the reach of our headlights. We can see remarkably far ahead, and to the sides as well. Note that clump of wild onions out there in the dark, and that blasted tree, and that jagged boulder stuffed into that trough of moss. And there, that little road marker no larger than a child's stone in a cemetery and which you refused to read.

But I will tell you something. The hour is precisely eighteen minutes past one a.m., and in mere moments, as soon as we are drawn into the gentleness of the long curve that lies just ahead—but of course it is still in- visible—there will be on our right a rather small grove of olive trees, a stone hut, a silent but watchful dog. And if you look when I tell you to look, you will see that among the olive trees someone has made a small pile of human possessions: a white wooden chair, a broken trunk, a crude rake for the garden, a heap of clothing that might have been stripped from dead bodies. It is difficult to understand that the life of the stone hut has been emptied into the darkness, and that the olive tree is beautiful only because it is so deformed. Yet these things are true.

travesty

It is amusing to think that tonight our speeding car shall frighten the abandoned dog.

But do you know that once Chantal and Honorine together urged me into the arms of a woman of luxury? It is true. Absolutely true. And I complied.

Chantal was only a girl at the time, and we were traveling, the three of us, in a car very like the one we are presently enjoying. We had dined well, after a day of gray clouds, flat road, high speed, and having left behind us connecting rooms with high ceilings, marble fireplaces, wallpaper the elegant color of dry bone, had walked into a moonlit street filled suddenly with the warmth of summer and the smell of flowers. A moving shadow, an open window, a few notes of music, and then we understood that we had stumbled into the very center of the honeyed hive of a city already acclaimed for its women. Down the narrow street we went arm in arm, laughing, Chantal and Honorine both claiming to be well-known residents of that gentle quarter. And I was in the middle, walking between Chantal and Honorine, and somewhere a caged bird was singing and even out there in the street I could smell fat bolsters, feather beds, nude flesh.

It was a night of wine. And the woman, when we found her, was much older than Honorine and might have come fresh from some turn-of-the-century stage

where whiteness of skin and heaviness of flesh and limb
were especially admired. Chantal and Honorine ex-
claimed their enchantment; I hesitated; the woman
raised her chin and smiled. And do you know that
Honorine proposed with so much good spirit that I
enjoy this woman that I became aroused and agreed to
leave Chantal and Honorine eating chocolates in a little
empty parlor while, several ornate rooms away, I contributed three quarters of an hour of sexual authenticity
to their delightful game? In taking that tall and heavy
woman, who filled her maturity with the exact same
elegance with which she lived in her skin, it was as if
I had only found my way again to Chantal and Honorine, and as if I had accepted from mother and daughter the same unimaginable gift. So I prepared the way
for you. Don't you agree? And with my two women,
who are yours as well, have I not created a family small
in size but rich in sentiment?

The next day we were a close and smiling triad as
we continued driving through the sterile marshlands
and past the great brown windmills with their sad faces
and broken arms.

But I must tell you that this little romantic story
about the complicity between my wife, my daughter,
and the older woman of luxury reminds me more
strongly than ever of a curious emotional reaction of
mine—a reaction I rarely recall and never felt except
upon one of those innumerable occasions of Chantal's
childhood happiness. That is, Chantal had only to re-

veal the slightest sign of personal enjoyment, had only
to pick some leaf or kiss Honorine or show me with
evident pleasure some faintly colored illustration in one
of her books, to send me sliding off into the oddest
kind of depression. I was a perfect companion to her
gloom, her anger, her hours of fear, her childhood pan-
tomimes of adult frustration, her little floods of helplessness in the face of some easy problem. But let Chantal throw her arms around my neck or grow warm of
cheek or simply give me a clue that she was momentarily alive in one of those private moments of beatitude
all children experience and I was hopelessly alien from
her and depressed, inexplicably downcast. Throughout
all of Chantal's childhood I was sorry for her whenever
I should have been glad. Yes, I was actually sorry for my
own child, but sorry only when she was in one of her
states of well-being. And when she was herself unhappy,
why then I was busily content.

I hear your impatience. And in the circumstances
my perhaps sentimental recollections must touch you
with profound irritation, especially since you have imagined so much more life than I myself have lived. And
perhaps you have already analyzed my darker, nearly
forgotten parental emotions as fear of mortality, and
have thus dismissed them. But I must ask you again to
indulge my nostalgia, if only because its source is gone,
quite gone, and I am now capable of loving Chantal
without putting myself perversely at the center of our
relationship, like the fat raisin that becomes the eye and

heart of the cookie. No, for years I have been what the rest of the world would call a normal father, feeling only joy for Chantal's joy and pain for her pain. My "perversion" has long since been cauterized. I no longer reverse and then exaggerate what Chantal feels. I still enjoy licking smeared chocolate from my daughter's fingers, and do so with perfect impunity. But I am in no way responsible for maintaining Chantal's life, and long ago gave up anticipating grief for its loss.

Do you know that now I am not even tempted to look into the rear-view mirror?

But there, the dashboard settings are now subtly different. You cannot be as aware of them as I am, yet for me the mere climbing or falling of needles, the sometimes monstrous metamorphosis of tiny, precise numbers behind faintly illuminated glass, a droplet traveling too quickly or too slowly through its fragile tube—these for me are the essential signs, the true language, always precious and treacherous at the same time. And now the settings are different. There are the mildest indications that we are beginning to deplete the resources of this superb machine, though in our present context those resources are of course inexhaustible and in fact will probably account for the grandeur of the sound that will wake our poor curate. Nonetheless the life of the car is running out, the end of our journey tonight is not as distant as one might think. Naturally there are steep grades, sudden turns, even abrasive changes in the road's surface, and still time enough to tax us, preoccupy us, demand the utmost from our living selves. And of course you may argue that our experience so far has been constant, virginal, that we have heard no variations in the music that reaches us from beneath the car; that Chantal has not discovered some poor wounded bird imponderably present and expiring on the seat beside her. Yes, things are the same, I am not even beginning to feel the strain of driving at this high speed.

But then our situation is not so very different from my war, as I call it, with Honorine's old-fashioned clock. It is a crude affair that hangs on her wall. Nothing but a few pieces of dark wood, a long cord with iron weights at either end, a circular ratchet, a horizontal pendulum fixed with wooden cubes like a tiny barbell. It is only the bare minimum of a clock, suggesting both the work of a child and the skill of some parsimonious medieval craftsman. Small, simple, dark, naked. And yet this contraption makes the loudest ticking I have ever heard. And slowly, it ticks more slowly, more firmly than any time device created by any of the old, bearded lovers of death in the high mountains. Well, I cannot stand that ticking. It is unbearable. So at every opportunity I stop the clock. But somehow it always starts up again and beats out its relentless unmusical strokes until once again I find it so insufferable that I jam its works.

You know the clock, you say? And you have never bothered to listen to the noise it makes? But of course you are familiar with Honorine's old clock. Of course you are. What a silly oversight. We are not strangers. Far from it. And how like you to be so unconcerned with something that gives me the utmost aural pain. But what I mean to say is this: that I hear that ticking loudest when the clock is stopped. Exactly. Exactly. It is the war I cannot win. But it is a lovely riddle.

The point is this: that our present situation is like my wife's old clock. The greater the silence, the louder the tick. For us the moment remains the same while the hour changes. And isn't it curious that I really know very little about automobiles? I merely drive them well.

Yes, it was a rabbit. You see it is true, as everyone says, that at high speeds you can feel absolutely nothing of the rabbit's death. But next it will rain, I suppose, as if an invisible camera were recording our desperate expressions through the wet glass. Perhaps you should have agreed to the radio after all.

Confession? Confession? But do you really believe that the three of us are sitting here in what I may call our exquisite tension (despite all my own pleasure in this event, I am not insensitive to the fact that we are in a way frozen together inside this warm automobile) merely so that I may indulge in guilty revelations and extract from you a few similar low-voiced scraps of broken narrative? No, *cher ami*, for the term "confession" let us substitute such a term as, say, "animated revery." Or even this phrase: "emotional expression stiffened with the bones of thought."

I do not believe in secrets—withheld or shared. Nor do I believe in guilt. At least let us agree that secrets and so-called guilty deeds are fictions created to enhance the sense of privacy, to feed enjoyment into our isolation, to enlarge the rhythm of what most people need, which is a belief in life. But surely "belief in life" is not for you, not for a poet. Even I have discovered the factitious quality of that idea.

No man is guilty of anything, whatever he does. There you have it. Secrets are for children and egotists and sensualists. Guilt is merely a pain that disappears as soon as we recognize the worst in us all. Absolution is an unnecessary and, further, incomprehensible concept. I am not attempting to justify myself or punish you. You are not guilty. Never for a moment did I think you were. As for me, my "worst" would not fill a crooked spoon.

And yet there are those of us, and I am doing my best to include you among our select few, for whom the most ordinary kind of daily existence partakes of the contradictory sensation we know as shame. For such people everything, everything, is eroticized. Such a man walks through the stalls of a butcher in a kind of inner heat, which accounts for his smile. But if we allow shame to the sensualist and deny guilt to the institutions, it is simply that such words and states serve poetic but not moral functions. In the hands of the true poet they are butterflies congregating high in the heavens, but in the hands of the moralists or the metaphysicians they are gunpowder.

But you are becoming angry, *cher ami*. Be patient.

Another cigarette. I approve. Though you must know that every minute you are growing more and more like my good but crippled doctor, despite the fact that you are in full possession of your four limbs. But it occurs to me that had I not given them up on the very day you entered our household, I would now ask you to reach slowly across the space between us and position your freshly lighted cigarette between my own dry lips. And you would do that for me. I know you would. And your shaking hand would hover there an instant just below my line of vision, sparing my own two hands for their necessary grip on the wheel, until I fished for the end of the cigarette with my parted lips and then found it, held it, inhaled. One of your cold fingers might even have brushed the tip of my nose as I waited and then exhaled, blowing one lungful of smoke against the inner side of the windshield like a silent wave curling along a glassy shore.

Cigarettes always make me think of bars. They

remind me of the war, of talkers around a dark table, of wine, of a woman's hand in my lap.

But no, not even that single puff. Not even now. It cannot be. And yet while you are drenched in the aroma of your cigarette, and while Chantal may be acquiring some slight awareness of the relative newness of this automobile which she cannot help but smell, I myself am breathing in fresh air, dead leaves, ripe grapes. And the windows are closed. Quite closed.

Chantal? Do you hear Papa's voice as through the ether? Whatever you are thinking, *ma cherie*, whatever monsters you may be struggling with, you must believe me that your presence here is not gratuitous. That would be the true humiliation, Chantal: to be as small as you are, to be as young as you are, to be seated behind Henri and me and hence quite alone in the car with no one to comfort you by touch or wordless embrace (precisely as I comforted you at the death of Honorine's Mama, that splended woman), and then to be conscious of yourself not only as so very different from the two men talking together in the front of this darkened and terribly fast sport touring car, but also to know yourself to be forgotten, only accidentally present, unwanted perhaps. What could be worse? Especially since you are in fact no child, and have spent almost the total store of your youthful sexuality on your own small portion of Henri's poetic vision, and since you

38

have always harbored a special regard for your Papa's love.

But it is not so, Chantal. You are no mere forgotten audience to the final ardent exchange between the two men in your mother's life, men whose faces you cannot even see. Not at all, Chantal. No, I have thought of you with utter faithfulness from the beginning. In my mind there were always three of us, Chantal, never two, and in all the accruing of the elements of this now inevitable event (the month, the day, the night, the route), there you were in the very center of my concern. And during these last hours it has been the same: when I thought of you and Henri finishing your dinner in the restaurant, when I waited for the attendant to go through the motions of pumping the last tankful of gasoline into this silent car, when I noticed on my wristwatch that the time of our rendezvous was approaching, even when I so unexpectedly depressed the accelerator and violently increased our speed and hence interrupted our lively conversation and signaled the true state of things: in all this you were the necessary third person whose importance was quite equal to Henri's and mine.

That the protective parent turns out to be the opposite, that familiar accord turns out to be the basket containing the hidden asp, that it is impossible to weigh the magnitude of what your father is doing as opposed to that of what will soon be happening—this is a disillusionment I cannot discuss for now. But let me at least reassure you in this other matter: you are here, now, with Henri and me, only because of the strength of my devotion, my poor Chantal. No one can rob you now of your Papa's love.

We are like the crow and the canary, *cher ami*. We are that different. And yet we are both Leos. It is almost enough to engage my interest in astrology. Or at least it is a fact that should help me to suppress more effectively my amusement at the new astrological age of the young. Of course this amusement of mine is more sympathetic than scornful: one cannot merely scoff at the signs of the zodiac sewn to the buttocks of the tight faded pants of our young men and women these days. How like them to believe in the old wizardry and yet sport these portentive signs so innocently, naïvely, on the seats of their pants.

But you and I are Leos. One more unbreakable thread in the web. What does it mean? Is it the crudest irony of all, or does it somehow light the way to our reconciliation? Is it a mockery of our differences or a hint as to the nature of that odd affinity for each other that we appear to share? Perhaps your future biographer will find in this astrological coincidence of ours the essential clue to what will always be known as your "untimely death." Who is to say?

I seem to remember an old adage that the true poet has the face of a criminal. And you have this

face. You and I know only too well that you are pub-
licly recognized by your short haircut, the whiteness of
your skin, the roughened texture of this white skin, the
eyes that are hard and yet at the same time wet and
always untrustworthy, as if they have been drained of
blueness in a black-and-white photograph. Are you beginning to see yourself, *cher ami?* Yours is the face of
the criminal, the lover from the lower classes, the face
of someone who has just died on a lumpy sofa in an
unfamiliar apartment and who lies there as if alive but
already cooling, with one hand touching the bare floor
and the grainy head supported in the grip of two cheap
sofa cushions. And no matter how you dress, whether
conventionally in your dark modest three-piece suit as
of this moment, attired in exactly that same absence
of flamboyance as myself, as if we had come from separate business offices only to meet on the same out-
moded train, or whether you are casually dressed in a
somewhat rumpled mauve shirt and loosened tie, as I
have often seen you, still for me you are only dressed
in one way: in black pants and in a white shirt that is
open at the collar, and tieless, and a little soiled. It is
the garb of the man about to be executed, the garb
of the unsmiling poet whose photograph is so often
taken among those festive crowds at the bull ring.

And let us not forget your days as a mental patient.
We are all familiar with those red-letter days of yours,
cher ami.

Yes, I know you well. Only a Leo could cultivate so

successfully this *persona* of the man who has emerged alive from the end of the tunnel or who has managed to cross the impossible width of the arena. It is always the same: you are like a man who spends his life in intense sunlight becoming all the while not pinker, darker, but only whiter, as if your existence is a matter of calculated survival, which accounts for your curious corpselike expression, which in turn is so appealing to women. You are plain, you smoke cigarettes, you appear to be the friend of at least half of all those professional *toreros* now working with the majestic bulls, as some people think of them.

And you have spent your days, months, in confinement. We have only to see your name, or better still to see your photograph or even catch a glimpse of you in person, to find ourselves confronting the bright sun, endless vistas of hot, parched sand, the spectacle of a man who always conveys the impression of having been dead and then joylessly resurrected—but resurrected nonetheless. Of course your suffering is your masculinity, or rather it is that illusion of understanding earned through boundless suffering that obtrudes itself in every instance of your being and that inspires such fear of you and admiration. Another way of putting it, is to say that you have done very well with hairy arms and a bad mood. But I am not trying to rouse you with insults. At any rate you will not deny that in yourself you have achieved that brilliant anomaly: the poet as eroticist and pragmatist combined. Though you merely write

travesty

poems, people admire you for your desperate courage. You are known for having discovered some kind of *mythos* of cruel detachment, which is another way of expressing the lion's courage. And I too am one of your admirers. Just think of it.

Your modesty? Honesty? Humility? Anxiety? I am aware of them all. In you these qualities are made of the same solid silver as that courage of yours. Yes, you are the kind of man who should always be accompanied by a woman who is the wife of a man as privileged as me. Only some such woman could qualify as your Muse and attest to your courage.

Well, I prefer the coward.

Is it possible then that I too am a Leo? I for whom the bull is interesting, if at all, not for his horns but for the disproportion between his large flabby hump and little hooves? I who possess none of those externals of personality which adorn you, *cher ami*, like *banderillas* stuck and swaying in the bull's hump? I who despise the pomp and frivolity of organized expiation? I for whom the window washer on a tall building is more worthy of attention than your *torero* in the moment of his gravest danger? I who must get along without a Muse and for whom poetry is still no match for journalistic exhibitionism? (The poetry of present company excluded, *cher ami*.)

Well, perhaps I am merely the product of an astrological error or, more likely, of some clerical slip in the mayor's office. Perhaps I am only a counterfeit Leo,

travesty

a person who has lived his life under the wrong sign
of the zodiac—the coward to your own man of courage.
But then how ironic it is that behind the wheel tonight
we find not the poet but only the man who disciplines
the child, carves the roast. Perhaps the crow is not so
inferior after all to his friend the canary.

It is quite true that I am unable to bear the cold. In
all her good humor, Honorine still considers it my se-
verest failing, this inevitable capitulation of mine to the
power of the falling thermometer. The shocking whiteness of our bed linen, the touch of approaching winter
on the back of my neck, the painful sensation of coldness spreading like water on tiles across the undersides
of my thighs, the chill my hand is forever detecting
on the surface of my rather bony chest (despite flannel
shirt, woolen pullover, tweed jacket), a sudden unpleasant deadening in the end of my nose—here is a
sensitivity which even I myself deplore. What could
be more cowardly than fear of the cold?

Yes, I fight the drafts. I complain bitterly indeed
about the trace of ice on the windowpane, the sound
of wind in our vaulted fireplace, the enemy that sets
the flame of the candle dancing. Do you know that I
suffer acutely because one of my ears is always colder
than the other? My feet begin to stiffen inside my thick
socks and English shoes, the coldness of my hands

defies the most vigorous rubbing, reproachfully I tell
Honorine that the walls are cold, that the fire is too
small, that someone has left one of our thick oaken
doors ajar. But you have heard my complaints. You
have even remarked that an old chateau is no place
for a man who sniffs out spiteful breezes in all seasons.

And yet you cannot know what it is to have cold
elbows. The elbows are the worst. Because in them the
little twin fiends of numbness and incapacity appear
to sit most easily, comfortably, as if the nearly naked
exposure of the bones in the elbows attracts most read-
ily those sensations—those two allegorical envoys—of
the ice that is already creeping and hardening across the
very surfaces of our last night. Oh yes, Honorine is tol-
erant of this obsessive susceptibility of mine. She is
forebearing, indulgent, good-humored, despite her crit-
ical comments and all these years of robes, hot fires,
the soft and warming fur of dead rabbits. And yet hours
after I have been restored as fully as possible to a condition resembling so-called normal body temperature,
it is then that I am most aware of the coldness lingering
in my elbows and of the fact that I can never be entirely
comfortable while for her part Honorine is never cold.
Actually, it is embarrassing to be unable to touch your
wife at night without first warming your hands in a
sinkful of scalding water. It is not pleasant to feel your
wife flinching even in the heat of her always sensible
and erotic generosity.

But I hope it is not too warm for you. Surely you

can understand that tonight especially the heating reg-
ulator is set precisely and, I admit, at the highest possible degree. In this case the discomfort you are being
made to feel is simply no match for that which I am
avoiding. Don't you agree?

So you think that I am merely deceiving you with
words. You think that I am trying to talk away the
last of our time together merely in order to destroy
the slightest possibility of my change of mind. You
think that I am shrouding the last dialogue of our
lives in the gauze of unreality, the snow of evasion. You
think that euphemism is my citadel, that all my poised
sentences are the work of mere self-protection, and
that if only you can persuade me to accept head-on
the validity of your word—that word—as the simplest
and clearest definition of the car accident that is intended and that involves persons other than the driver,
then you will have won the very reprieve which, from
the start, I have tried to convince you does not exist.
Well, beware, *cher ami*. Beware.

But perhaps you are right. Perhaps "murder" is
the proper word, though it offends my ear as well as
my intentions. However, mine is not a fixed and predictable personality, and you may be right. I too am
open to new ideas. So let us agree that "murder" is
at least a possibility. Let us hold it in store, so to

46

speak, for the final straightaway. But I ask only that you then find new and more pertinent connotations of that ugly word and make your most objective effort to believe—believe—that there can be no exceptions to the stages, as I've sketched them, of what we may call our private apocalypse. It is like a game: I cannot accept the idea of "murder" unless you are able to refuse the illusory comfort of "reprieve." After all, how can the two of us talk together unless you are fully aware that the two of us are leaping together, so to speak, from the same bridge?

Which reminds me of a singular episode of my early manhood. It occurred when Honorine was hardly more than a seductive silhouette on my black horizon. And yet it was most instructive, this brief event, and may well be the clue to the beginning of my romantic liaison with Honorine and even to the lasting strength of my marriage. Certainly it determined or revealed the nature of the life I would lead henceforth as well as the nature of the man I had just become. It is something of a travesty, involving a car, an old poet, and a little girl. Perhaps we shall get to it. Perhaps. For now you must simply believe me when I say that, thanks to this singular episode, my own early manhood contained its moment of creativity. In my youth I also had my taste or two of that "cruel detachment" which was to make you famous. More similarities between the canary and his friend the crow. But now you must realize that you have always underestimated the diversity, as we may call it, of the members of the privileged class.

At least you have always appreciated Honorine. Yet who would not? In her entire person is she not precisely the incarnation of everything we least expect to find in the woman who appears to reveal herself completely, and no matter how attractively, in the first glance? Think of her now, not sleeping in that massive antique bed of hers, but, say, outdoors and bending to her roses or better, perhaps, in our great hall and sitting on her leather divan and wearing her tight plum-colored velvet slacks and white linen blouse. Only another attractive, youthful-looking married woman of the privileged class, we assume. Only one of those conventional women framed, so to speak, by her bankbook and happy children and a car of her own. We see her against a background of yellow cloth on which has been imprinted a tasteful arrangement of tree trunks and little birds; we know that everything in her domain reflects a pleasing light, a texture of familiar elegance; we recognize that she is neither large nor small, neither beautiful nor plain, despite her golden hair cut short and feathery in the mode of the day; we expect her to be little more than a kindly person, a friend to other

travesty

women, a happy mother, a fair athlete, someone who reads books and supervises the redecoration of an old chateau and secretly tries to imagine a better life. Large but studious-looking eyeglasses of yellowish shell, shoes that gleam with the aesthetic richness of the country from which they have been imported, a wedding band excessively studded with rare stones, an agreeable mind that complements the oval face, the willing personality that reflects the hot bath taken only moments before—all these telltale signs we both have scanned too often in the past, have we not? Haven't we here the young middle-aged woman who cannot quite compete with the paid models in the fashion magazine but who yet catches our eye? The young matron not quite distinguished enough to join the striking matriarch on the facing page, yet benign enough to make us think of a drop of honey on a flat square of glass? If this is she —the woman in tennis shorts, the person who smiles, the wife with trim legs in which the veins are beginning to show—then we have seen her kind before and cannot find her especially interesting. Everything about such a person suggests the bearded father, the hand prepared well in advance to tend the sumptuous roses, a certain intelligence in the eyes, but finally the undeniable indications of the female life that is destined, after all, for unfulfillment—which is not interesting. No, we are hardly about to spend time or undertake the risks of seduction for a mere drop of honey on a sheet of glass. Let her remain in her old chateau where she belongs, surrounded as she deserves to be by husband and children and all of her uncertain advantages. At best this woman will give us only pride or pathos, being too long descended, as she appears to be, from that original countess who in ageless vigor maintained who knows what naked dominion in the boudoir.

But how wrong it all is, how very wrong. Superficially correct, and yet totally wrong. Yes, you and I know better, do we not? Together we know that the beauty of our Honorine is that, deserving these various epithets as she surely does, still she contains within herself precisely the discretion and charm and sensual certainty we could not have imagined. On this you will bear me out. I know you will.

Just think of it: you sit beside her on the cream-colored leather divan; you remove the owlish eyeglasses and notice that the eyes are flecked in the corners with anxiety; the great hall is silent, waxen, filled with the residual afterglow of the late sun; you notice that the face turned in your direction is strong but that the smile could be interpreted as timid; your hand grazes the chaste white linen of the blouse which, her eyes still on yours, her body apparently relaxed, she herself begins to unbutton, as if without thinking; with relief you notice an endearing tobacco stain on several of the otherwise conventionally white teeth; and then like a figure from our wealth of erotic literature, you find yourself kneeling on that polished stone floor and holding a firm ankle in one hand and in the other the heel of a shoe that appears to have been molded from dark chocolate. And then she leans forward, leans on your shoulder, frees herself of the shoes you could not remove, and then stands up and, for a moment, experiences girlish difficulty with the zipper of the plum-colored velvet pants. Well, the vision is yours as well as mine: the disappearance of the velvet trousers, the strength and shapeliness of the hands that pull down the underpants, the clear uncertain tone of the voice in which she remarks (quite wrongly, as all of my photographs attest) that she has never been very good at stripping. And there at eye level, for you are still kneeling, there at eye level we find the slight protrusion of the hip bone, the modest appearance of the secret hair which might have been shaven but was not, the smallest off-center appearance of the navel born of the merest touch of a hot iron against that soft and ordinary flesh. But more, much more, as only you and I could know. Because just there, adorning that small area between navel and pubic hair, there you see once again the cluster of pale purple grapes on yellow stems—yellow stems!—that coils down from the navel of our Honorine or, to put it another way, that crowns the erogenous contours of our Honorine as it did even when she was only an unexpectedly eccentric girl. Grapes, *cher ami*, a tattoo of smoky grapes that move when she breathes or whenever there is the slightest spasm or undulation in her abdomen. After seeing them, who would risk any constricting definition of our Honorine?

travesty

But you and I have been the foxes to those ripe grapes, have we not? And to think that it is she, this sleeping Honorine, who awaits our passing.

Well, now you can breathe again, as can I. That's a dangerous turn, you saw how much trouble it gave me, for all my knowledge of our route and no matter the perfect timing—or perhaps nearly perfect timing, I should say—with which I prepared once more to meet its treachery. Yes, an extremely difficult turn, a threatening moment indeed, as you could tell by the song of our tires and my silence and the sternness with which I held the wheel. Of course you too felt that sudden inundation of centrifugal force, the nausea that told us that we might in fact be leaving the road. But it's all right, the uncertainty is past, we have emerged from the turn, again we are safely adhering to the earthly path of our trajectory—which on a white road map looks exactly like the head of a dragon outlined by the point of a pen brutally sharpened and dipped in blood. But it is precisely by such small incidents as this one, when all at once the irrationality of the night intrudes upon us, that we inside the car are given to see ourselves as through the eyes of some old sleepless goatherd on a distant hill: to him, we are only the brief inaccessible stab of light that announces impersonally —quite impersonally—the vicious passing of an invisible and even inconsequential automobile through the damp and chilly medium of the black night. Then we are gone.

And so we are. So we are.

Chantal? Can it be? Have you forgotten the injunction of your Papa? Have you, like a poor childish sleepwalker, slipped free of your belt and worked your way down, down to the narrow but thickly carpeted area between the rear seat and two front seats? You, Chantal, burrowing down back there like some little frightened animal or tearful child? But it is a grievous tabloidal gesture. It could hardly be more hurtful to your Papa, who despairs to imagine you now conscious of nothing whatsoever except the burden of your own pure and quite meaningless revulsion. It is not how I thought you would behave, Chantal. Surely you cannot hope to save yourself by lying flat or in the fetal position and bracing yourself with knees and shoulders and covering your distracted face with your beautiful, small hands? Alas, the effort is futile, as you must know. But perhaps you are simply trying to escape your Papa's voice. Could it be that? You prefer the fine soft music of our transmission to the truth of what your Papa is saying? But there is time yet to recover yourself and regain your seat and participate in the assessment, analysis, of our discussion.

travesty

After all, you are nearly twenty-five years old. And I confess I found your sobbing more tolerable than this sudden convulsive state of withdrawal. But can't you see that this collapse of yours is, at the very least, an extreme distraction? Think of it, Chantal, we may not be so fortunate on the next turn.

But here it is, *cher ami:* my own dear Chantal lying face down behind us. How much worse it is for my poor child than I imagined. And only a few days ago I watched from our bedroom window as below in the otherwise empty courtyard Chantal, fresh from her riding lesson and dressed in her whipcord britches and black boots, emerged from this very automobile, alone except for her mother's Afghan which she was holding on a leather leash. The cobblestones like loaves of moldy bread, the long beige-colored car, the dog with his silken brown and white coat ruffling in the afternoon's cool breeze, the small and quick-moving woman with her dark hair, olive complexion, black riding boots, and dwarfed by the dog—it was a sight I could not help but admire, safe as I was from the long waves of regret which that same scene would have inspired in me in years past. I was still aware that Chantal's energetic presence below in the courtyard only heightened all the more the abandoned quality I especially appreciate in my wife's chateau, as if one could catch a glimpse of a large modern car left standing empty inside the iron gates of the very castle where the sleeping princess lies in all her pallor. I thought of it from my place at the window. But what most held my attention was the sheer vigor of the young woman below with the dog. How tight she was in her small body, I thought, and in her dark complexion how very different she was from our own fair and slowly sauntering Honorine. Yes, Chantal takes her small size and rose-and-olive beauty from her grandmother, that woman of diminutive regal shape and Roman coloring. How odd that not a trace of the old woman's alluring decadence is to be found in the features of our Honorine.

But now she has collapsed, the "porno brat" who became my child of the Renaissance. A few days ago I watched her crossing the courtyard quickly, happily, somewhat disheveled from her ride. The tall thin dog drifted from view to the clicking of my daughter's boot heels. She abandoned the car, this car, with the door on the driver's side wide open. I smiled. Now Chantal lies behind us, her body crumpled on the floor of the car like the corpse of an abducted socialite. She is a cameo nearly destroyed. And yet need I say that regret is not at all the same as grief?

I have two significant regrets. Only two. The first is that the crash soon to be reported as having occurred near the little village of La Roche must result inevitably in fire; the second is that the remains of the crash must inevitably disappear.

travesty

No doubt such considerations are not important. Even now I can hear your argument that these refinements of mine are for you nothing more than trivia elevated to the condition of impossible torment, or that at a time like this my extensive articulation of violent, unseemly details is nothing more than a kind of unfair tugging on the fishhooks already embedded beneath your skin. But of course I would by no means accept the notion of "trivia"; the nature and extent of physical damage can never be trivial, even when measured against the irreplaceable loss of three lives. And surely I need not remind you that I am serious and hence not at all interested in the infliction of minor psychological injury. On the other hand, if you were in fact thinking, if you were but a little more engaged in our discussion, then you might well retort that for a man who has pre-empted absolute or, we might say, whiplash control over this much immediate last-minute life, all speculative fantasy becomes a mere glut of self-indulgence. What, you ask, is he not satisfied with things as they are, with all the tangible evidence of the terrible blow he is dealing his daughter, his closest friend, himself, but what he must inflate himself still further and so must invent in his own eyes, arrange within his own head, even that context of circumstances in which the three of us will no longer exist? But he goes too far, you say, too far. Well, it would be a pretty speech if you could make it. But even if you did reply to me with some such dubious form of logic, my own reply, prompt

56

and good-natured as it would clearly be, would convince even you that it is this idea precisely that lies at the dead center of our night together: that nothing is more important than the existence of what does not exist; that I would rather see two shadows flickering inside the head than all your flaming sunrises set end to end. There you have it, the theory to which I hold as does the wasp to his dart. Without it, we would have no choice but to diffuse the last of our time together by passing between us the fuming bottle of cognac bought and freshly opened for just this occasion. But thanks to my theory we are spared such an intolerable waste. There shall be no slow maudlin loss of consciousness for you, for me. After all, my theory tells us that ours is the power to invent the very world we are quitting. Yes, the power to invent the very world we are quitting. It is as if the bird could die in flight. And unless we exercise this power of ours we merely slide toward the pit feet first, eyes closed, slack, and smiling in our pathetic submission to an oblivion we still hope to understand. But for us it will be different, *cher ami.* Quite different.

And yet I must say it. I regret the fire. Here even I am helpless. My theory does not apply to exploding gasoline. And I am sure that you will appreciate the fact that my attitude toward the burning of our demolished car has nothing to do with any personal feeling of mine against roadside cremation. On that score I am indifferent. But if I were able to prevent that burst of flame, to obliterate the sparks before their very inception and so stop the hot flame, the sheet of light, the fire that will turn to brightness the entire area of wall, wreckage, gasoline spreading and thus extending still further the circle of this most intense visibility—yes, if I could eliminate the flames I would. Yes, it seems to me that if we preserve this scene in all its magnitude and with all its confounding of disparate substances and with its same volume of sound, but remove from it the convention of fierce heat and unnaturally bright light, so that this very explosion occurs as planned but in darkness, total darkness, there you have the most desirable rendering of our private apocalypse. Announced by violent sound and yet invisible, except for the glass scattered like perfect clear grains across an entire field —what splendor, what a perfect overturning of ordinary expectation. The unseen vision is not to be improved upon.

Well, you will understand that in much the same way I would prefer that the remains of our crash go undiscovered, at least initially. I would prefer that these remains be left unknown to anyone and hence unexplored, untouched. In this case we have at the outset the shattering that occurs in utter darkness, then the first sunrise in which the chaos, the physical disarray, has not yet settled—bits of metal expanding, contracting, tufts of upholstery exposed to the air, an unsocketed dial impossibly squeaking in a clump of thorns— though this same baffling tangle of springs, jagged edges

travesty

of steel, curves of aluminum, has already received its
first coating of white frost. In the course of the first
day the gasoline evaporates, the engine oil begins to
fade into the earth, the broken lens of a far-flung head-
light reflects the progress of the sun from a furrow in
what was once a field of corn. The birds do not sing,
clouds pass, the wreckage is warmed, the human remains are integral with the remains of rubber, glass,
steel. A stone has lodged in the engine block, the process of rusting has begun. And then darkness, a cold
wind, a shred of clothing fluttering where it is snagged
on one of the doors which, quite unscathed, lies flat
in the grass. And then daylight, changing temperature,
a night of cold rain, the short-lived presence of a scav-
enging rodent. And despite all this chemistry of time,
nothing has disturbed the essential integrity of our
tableau of chaos, the point being that if design inevitably surrenders to debris, debris inevitably reveals its
innate design. Until one day two boys stumble upon
the incongruity of a once beautiful automobile smashed
in the barnyard of an abandoned farm. For them the
spectacle yields only delight: a little plastic-coated iden-
tity card winking in the sunlight, dead leaves nesting in
the wheels which lie on their sides, a green shoot growing from the mouth of the rusty and half-crumpled fuel
tank. Indeed, this spectacle now exists merely for them,
merely for the pleasure of two boys in ill-fitting trousers
and wooden shoes. But who better might we have as
witnesses?

travesty

Well, it is impossible. It is not to be. Nothing will prevent our sudden incandescence in the night sky. And then we shall have blue lights, motorcycles, radio communications, the arrival of several of our little white ambulances. By dawn they will be hauling apart our wreckage with hooks and chains, and by noon of that first day there will be nothing left but the smell of gasoline and the dark signs of a recently extinguished fire. They will make notes, take photographs, climb through the elbows of hot metal, and then tow it all away with their clumsy trucks.

How sad it is, *cher ami*. What a brutal sport.

Perhaps if you make an effort to remain still, to position your arms so as to allow your chest room enough for its greatest possible expansion, and then breathe in slow conscious cadences through your open mouth, perhaps if you undertake these measures you will be more comfortable. But it is an unfortunate development, this partial suffocation resulting from that dreadful constricting of the bronchial tubes. I can imagine the growing panic of not being able to breathe, *cher ami*. You have my sympathies. Apparently your various nervous and physiological systems are quite de-determined not to be outdone by all the failures, impairments, of our poor Chantal. Now that the seizure is upon you, so to speak, I do remember your bitter

travesty

description of yourself as an infrequent but nonetheless violent sufferer of this diabolical chest affliction. Generally it is a childhood illness, is it not? But the unfortunately unavoidable extremity of artificial heat, the closeness of the air around us, the effect of your cigarettes on a chest condition as sensitive as this one is, and of course the severe emotionalism of your present state —no doubt all this is conducive to one of your infrequent attacks, as you call them, of thick and heavily labored breathing. And then the whole thing is circular, is it not? The greater the pain, the greater the weight bearing down on your chest, the louder that dreadful rasping sound (it is indeed a curiously annoying sound, *cher ami*), the greater your own fury which, being directed at the self, of course, only gives still greater impetus to the whole wheezing machine.

Well, you have my sympathies. The onset of this condition of yours, with its promise of facial discoloration and even loss of consciousness so evident in every rattling breath you take, must certainly come as the final outrage, like eczema on top of leprosy. And unless I am mistaken, by now you are quite wet with perspiration. I suppose the body expresses what the mind refuses to tolerate, which probably says something about my own single lung and satisfactory respiratory system. But I would give you relief if it were in my power. Fields of oxygen, the smell of a blue sky. . . . I wish I could give them to you, *cher ami*. As it is, I am certainly going to find it harder to hear your voice, while for you

it will be much more difficult to concentrate on anything but these increasing indications of expiring breath.
But perhaps you should remember that it is only the
rarest person who is not in one sense or another gasp-
ing for air.

Our villages carved out of old bone, our forests
shimmering with leaves the color of dried tobacco, our
village walls over which the dead vines are draped like
fishing nets, the weight of the stones that occupy the
slopes of our barren hills like sculpted sheep, the smell
of wood smoke, the ruby color of wine held to the natural light, the white pigeon drawn to the spit even as
he becomes aroused on the rim of the fountain—surely
there is no eroticism to match the landscape of spent
passion. There is nothing like an empty grave to betray
the presence of a dead king in all his lechery. The
blasted tree contains its heart of amber, you can smell
the wild roses in the sterile crevices of ancient cliffs,
suddenly you find the whitened limb of a tree sleeved
in green. Yes, ours is a landscape of indifferent hunters
and vanished lovers, *cher ami,* so that but to exist
on such a terrain, aware of blood and manure, of the
little paper sacks of poison placed side by side with
bowls of flowers on the window ledges of each village
street, or aware of the unshaven faces of our local
pharmacists or of the untended pubescence of the girls

who work in our markets and confess their fantasies in our darkened churches—yes, simply to exist in such a world is to be filled with a pessimism indistinguishable from the most obvious state of sexual excitation. I am a city person and not without my own form of pragmatism. And yet whenever I have seen from the window of this very car a glimpse of a distant woodland, I have thought of the royal hunting party mounted and in pursuit of a fevered stag, and thought of the sound of the horns, the lovers in that boisterous army, pretty and plumed, flushed and separated on their tossing horses but riding only in wait for the day of the chase to give way to the night of the tryst, when the mouth that took the brazen hunting horn by day will take the elegant and ready flesh by night. Yes, we who are the gourmets and amateur excavators of our cultural heritage know in our cars, our railway trains, our pretentious establishments of business, that we have only to pause an instant in order to unearth the plump bird seasoning on the end of its slender cord tied to a rafter, or a fat white regal chamber pot glazed with the pastel images of decorous lovers, or a cracked and dusty leather boot into which some young lewd and brawny peasant once vomited.

Yes, dead passion is the most satisfying, *cher ami*. You have hinted as much in your verses. But no wonder I have always thought of Honorine as mistress of a small chateau and nude beneath a severe black hunting costume for riding sidesaddle, though she has never been on a horse in her life. And you can imagine my pleasure when Honorine did in fact inherit from her mother, that noble woman, the small chateau which I myself named Tara and which you and I have filled with the deadest of all possible passion. You don't agree? You disclaim anything but vitality and tenderness in your relations with Chantal and Honorine? Then perhaps it is only my own passion that is so very dead, *cher ami.*

But the owl is watching us. And look there. Rain. Just as I expected. Soon the invisible camera will be trained on us through the wet and distorting lens of our windshield.

But I too once had a mistress. You did not know? Well, I hope that despite all you have been told about the power of your sullen allure you do not consider yourself the only person to have received the gift of love as seen through the prism, as I may call it, of another woman, though it is true that my own experience was confined to a single mistress and not to a pair. Never in my lifetime would I have contemplated a pair of mistresses. I am one of those lesser and hence more limited men, as you well know.

But little Monique was quite enough for me at the time. At the beginning of our friendship she was only a few weeks into her twentieth year, which, come to

think of it, was exactly Chantal's age when you, in all
your mysterious naturalness and unconcern, determined to extend to her the love of the poet, if you will
indulge the expression. Then too, Monique was a shade
smaller even than Chantal, a fact I take to mean not
that I was trying to duplicate my daughter in my mistress but simply that I was lucky enough to win Monique
with a single glance and that she was the smallest person with whom I ever shared what she used to call
the dialogue of the skin. Her size was important to me
not because it mimed specifically the small size of
Chantal and Chantal's lovely grandmother, but only
because it bore out so perfectly an idea that has ob-
sessed me since earliest manhood: that the smaller the
woman one regards the greater one's amazement at
the vastness, fierceness, of the human will.

So Monique was remarkable, then, for her startling
size, the utter harmony of her physical proportions, the
immensity and even dangerous quality of her will. Her
self-assertiveness was staggering. Of course she never
failed to obey me, and yet even when she conformed
to my simplest suggestion (about what to eat, what not
to eat, some article of clothing, and so forth) she did
so with beautiful vehemence, as if she were acting on
her own prideful volition instead of mine. But never
fear, she gave as good as she received.

If I loved Monique for her size, I loved her equally
for the nature of her skin and its complexion. Tight,
painfully and wonderfully tight over the entirety of her

little face and limbs and torso, so thin and tight that actually I used to fear the consequences of a slip of the threaded needle. And of course her skin was white, almost glazed, in fact, and whiter even than Honorine's fair skin. And you know that my predilection for whiteness is just as intense as my appreciation of the Mediterranean hues.

Short skirts, short hair, bright blue lacquered shoes, occasionally a blouse tastefully crocheted, and the inevitable silk stockings as if always to confirm her threatened womanhood—I can still see her, one of the most inventive girls and strongest human beings I have ever known. I used to meet her twice a month on a schedule so strict that it did not vary more than several minutes from one occasion to the next. We were equally intolerant of lateness, though the flowers I carried and the luxury of the car I drove always gave me the advantage in these matters of time and demonstrations of anger. But we enjoyed each other's anger, and vied with each other in the creation of embarrassing public displays of bad temper. It was as if we shared between us an unspoken agreement to parody the lovers' quarrel, the domestic disagreement, whenever possible. Yes, even now it gives me oddly pleasurable satisfaction to recall how often I submitted to the insults she shouted at me on the most crowded of street corners (in the sun, in the rain, in the darkness after a splendid meal), and how she in her turn bore with quivering fury the disciplinary blows I so often inflicted with the edge of my heavy fork on her fragile wrist, usually under the eager eyes of an old waiter in the most elegant of restaurants. But as I say, it is a familiar and convenient pattern, this happy ritual of disruption and reconciliation. We relied on it totally, Monique and I.

At any rate Monique was proud, opinionated, hostile, inventive. It never failed to delight me that she could be so cruel of tongue, so vicious, or that a chest as small as hers was capable of such heavy breathing, or that she could become so quickly subdued and smaller than ever once seated in the rich interior of my powerful and highly polished car. But let me tell you that this Monique, whose youth and personality were so impressive, nonetheless and of her own free choice was the living example of all the uninhibited nudes I courted in the pornographic magazines of my own late and isolated boyhood. Not only was she a natural actress in the theater of sex, not only did she become in her mind and body the very flesh and activity of all those distant uncountable images of mine, but on top of everything else she collected in her small overfurnished rooms every conceivable kind of pornographic or erotic book, magazine, photograph that she was able to discover in our museums, kiosks, bookstalls, establishments devoted to the equipment and stimulation of the sexual drive. She lived her very life in unwitting competition with that rare photographic study which I prepared over the years of Honorine's own erotic womanhood. But Monique's performances were cruder, much cruder, than my study of Honorine. And at times they suddenly revealed my young friend's sense of humor, whereas there was no place for humor in my nude or partially nude views of Honorine.

Quick to take offense, quick to become aroused, quick to laugh at herself and at such exaggerated sexual animation in one so small—there we have our tireless Monique, who thrived on her pornography old and new and liked nothing better than to adorn her own little nude figure in the outlandish black lingerie of those ladies of the boas who in another era so incensed our forefathers. Yes, she collected and wore all those belts and harnesses and spangled black stockings as avidly as she immersed herself in her books and magazines. And do you know, *cher ami,* she had a palate that demanded only the finest of white wines. Only the finest.

But then there came at last that warm spring night when, suddenly inspired, I spanked Monique. It was not entirely my fault, and it was the only time in my life when I fell so close to being the sadistic villain lurking everywhere in the stories, photographs and fantasies of my little mistress. You will agree that no one wants to find himself becoming nothing more than a familiar type created by a hasty and untalented pornographer. We do not like to think of ourselves as imaginary, salacious and merely one of the ciphers in the bestial horde, to put it somewhat strongly, *cher ami.* But it was not totally my fault, as I must repeat, since the night was rainy and since the hour was late and since there was provocation, a provocation I did not even think to resist.

Well, you have the picture: spring rain, the city sleeping in its tile and stones, a wash of faint light from a bulb in a rose-colored shade, the warm little room smelling of the new season and of the oil of peach seeds with which Monique had scented her hot douche, and of course the two of us lying nude among the bolsters (except for Monique, who was wearing one of her scanty black harnesses known in the parlance of our grand temptresses as a garter belt). There you have it: the small, young, nearly naked girl on her stomach, the stockings which she had already removed adrift on the floor, the two of us slowly passing between us a set of large new photographs as rich and stimulating as ripened cheese. It was a scene that might have come directly from the writing desk or cold and shabby studio on one of our poor, dull, unshaven pornographers.

But as I have been saying, I had not the slightest thought of causing Monique even a moment of pain that night; I was not unusually aware of her childish, upturned buttocks twitching occasionally in the rose-colored suffusion from the lamp in the corner; I felt no need to exert any special mastery over Monique amidst the muffling softness of so many tasteless (but appropriate) oriental bolsters. And yet when all at once the moment of provocation was upon me, and in fact it was nothing more than a pouting underlip and some sort of pert, injurious remark quite lost now to passing time, it was then that I knew without any hesitation that I wanted to spank Monique—and to spank her in the conventional position, with my bare hand, with conscious determination and as hard and as long as possible. Mind you, until that instant I was absolutely uninitiated into that commonplace practice of familial punishment. And yet I did not hesitate, it did not occur to me to spare Monique one trace of humiliation or one grain of pain: I was not interested in justice or the possible sexual consequences of that event. To the contrary, thought and action were as one and I seized Monique abruptly, joyously, and like a vindictive father of long experience pulled my little startled mistress across my naked lap where I held that sprawled and squirming body in a grip that made escape impossible. The pleasure of the first long, deliberate blow was immense. Simply immense.

Well, the palm of my hand was a cruel and relentless paddle. Monique cried out, I gave not a thought to the sleeping neighbors, I spanked Monique with a lack of restraint astonishing even to myself. It was as if I could not bring the flat of my hand into hurtful contact with the soft, private world of her buttocks often enough or hard enough, so that I increased my efforts and gave myself total consciousness of touch and sound and enjoyed to the fullest the agitation of her helplessness. And then breathless, delighted, feeling the heat in my hand and a sparkling sensation throughout my own nakedness, finally I stopped. Only then did she cease resisting. Only then did she go limp, roll slowly away from me, and smother her angry sobs in one of the bolsters. Her weeping was a shameless exploitation of her childlike appearance, but it was an agreeable addition to the pleasure I was then savoring in my exhaustion.

So I myself fell back among the bolsters, surprised at what had happened but smiling, hearing the rain, feeling my own body filled, as it were, with crystals of vigor. Partially on my side and in a condition of curious alertness, peacefully I contemplated the body lying in rare quiescence and with its back to me. Yes, the buttocks were still pink, and pinker yet because of the lampshade. Every now and again a tremor passed down the spine or through one slender leg as if, released from my grip, she was striving now to relieve the discomfort of her small *derrière* by settling her body more deeply into the rolling, Oriental softness. The spare, black, lacy harness was low and loose on her little hips, one of her hands crept back and of its own accord began to rub and soothe the afflicted area. I watched her, I smiled. I did not for a moment think I had done any genuine harm. It even occurred to me, and with reason, that Monique in her sobbing was actually just as expectant as I was in my smiling. Of course by now my great bird, if you will allow the poetic license, was soaring in flight, so that it was only natural that while I watched Monique's small hand moving to pacify the hurt in her buttocks, my own firm hand—the very one with which I had performed what she later called the abomination—became a skilled and willing communicant with my distended sex.

How long we were held together in that wordless state of sexual torpor I do not know. Only the movements of our hands, fingers, suggested that even we two nude luxuriating figures lay under the spell of time. But then Monique herself effected the transition to what would lead, or so I quite wrongly thought, to our embrace. She turned her head and looked at me. One moment I was merely the comfortable *voyeur* who in actuality sees very little, the next I was looking directly into the small, handsome face of my Monique and growing suddenly expansive at the sight of the tears on the cheeks, the wet nose, the familiar, hard, dark scrutiny which I seemed to detect in the filmy eyes. Yes, I felt that now I was performing, so to speak, not merely for myself but for Monique's own attentive contemplation. She was watching me, she was waiting, I thought that in a moment she would creep to my arms.

But how wrong I was. Because even now and betraying not the slightest sign of her intention, Monique was already preparing herself to become like nothing so much as a cat in a sack. She smiled, I felt forgiven. In a spasm of her former childish energy she was on all fours, I rose on an expectant elbow. She leapt to her feet on the floor and struck and held a suggestive pose, I responded with more explicit and vigorous manipulation. She stripped off the little black threatening belt, in eager anticipation I sat up and held out one beckoning arm to her. She raised the belt above her head (rather than tossing it away as I thought she would), and even then I merely exposed myself still further to what I thought was going to be some new form of erotic stimulation. Would you believe it?

Even when I beheld and felt the first lash across my thighs, I thought she meant only to whip me lightly to ejaculation, a process, which, at that moment, I imagined as a fulsome and brilliant novelty. But when I received the second lash, this time across the eyes so that instinctively I covered my face with both my arms, and then received full in the lap the pain of the little metal grips affixed to the tips of those four silken straps, of course I realized that she meant quite the opposite.

Yes, with terrible precision and on an ascending scale of strength and tempo, my little mistress thrashed me on face and lap, chest and lap, until I thought the very possibility of sexual discharge was no longer mine. I groaned, I tasted blood, I cowered. My great bird was dead. And yet throughout the ordeal, while attempting hopelessly to protect myself, still I was somehow admiringly aware of the legs apart, the dark flashing eyes, the vindictive, animated dance of that small, nude girl, the black straps that flew from her fist like the snakes from the head of some tiny and gloriously tormented Medusa. She flayed me. She did so with joy. And even that was not the end of it.

Because when at last she stopped, not from fatigue but from an unbearable excess of exhilaration, she flung the now useless garter belt into the very lap she had but a moment before so fiercely beaten. It was a gesture of superb contempt. But as if that gesture of contempt were not enough, for an instant she looked around the room helplessly, trapped in the passion of her distraction and clear purpose, and then in wickedness and exasperation flung herself down beside me among the bolsters and with the furious fingers of both hands brought herself to an orgasm that would have satisfied even a cat in a sack. At least it satisfied Monique. In my defeat and discomfort I too felt a certain relief, a certain happiness for Monique, and if in the midst of helplessness and pain I had nonetheless been able to photograph her benign expression, surely I would have set up the tripod, triggered the blinding light. As it was I merely gave myself to the sound of the rain and finally, on all fours, made my way to my clothes.

Well, it was an instructive night, as you can see. An hour, two hours, and as from nothing a new bond of accord was suddenly drawn between Monique and myself. I learned that I too had a sadistic capacity and that the commiseration of Honorine was even vaster and sweeter than I had thought. But what is still most important about that particular and now long-lost night is that it reveals that I too have suffered and that I am not always in total mastery of the life I create, as I have been accused of being. Furthermore it illustrates that I am indeed a specialist on the subject of dead passion. At any rate, and for better or worse, I abandoned Monique when you entered our household. Somehow your presence made Monique's unnecessary. But of course there are moments, such as this one, when she still dances inside my head with a vividness quite comparable to that of the life enclosed within our own small world which is moving—need I say it?—with the speed and elasticity of the panther in full chase.

I am always moving. I am forever transporting myself somewhere else. I am never exactly where I am. Tonight, for instance, we are traveling one road but also many, as if we cannot take a single step without discovering five of our own footprints already ahead of us. According to Honorine this is my other greatest failing or most dangerous quality, this propensity of mine toward total coherence, which leads me to see in one face the configurations of yet another, or to enter rose-scented rooms three at a time, or to live so closely to the edge of likenesses as to be eating the fruit, so to speak, while growing it. In this sense there is nowhere I have not been, nothing I have not already done, no person I have not known before. But then of course we have the corollary, so that everything known to me remains unknown, so that my own footfalls sound like those of a stranger, while the corridor to the lavatory off my bedroom suddenly becomes the labyrinthine way to a dungeon. For me the familiar and unfamiliar lie everywhere together, like two enormous faces back to back. I am always seeing the man in the child, the child in the grown man. Winter is my time of flowers, I am a resigned but spirited voyager. Of course the whole thing is only a kind of psychic slippage, an interesting trick of *déjà vu,* although Honorine insists that it is a form of mystical insight. She is inclined to idealize me in her own reasonable and admirable fashion. But then I must add that at certain times she has found my mental disappearances, as she calls them, not merely disconcerting but fearful. And yet I have never given Honorine literal cause for anxiety, I can promise you that. She will be the last to propose any ready answers when she learns what has become of us tonight.

But no doubt I have been meaning to say that every more or less privileged person contains within himself the seed of the poet, so that the wife of each such individual wants nothing more than to be a poet's mistress. In this respect Honorine has been especially fortunate.

Do not be alarmed, *cher ami.* The matter at hand is not necessarily so very important. But we might as well spare ourselves whenever we can. The problem is that there is exactly time enough for me to forewarn you that in a few seconds we will be passing directly through the center of the only village that lies between the beginning of our trip tonight and its conclusion, and that mars an otherwise quite empty road. The little place is known for its ruined abbey, or perhaps it is a ruined mill. But believe me, please. This route was the most fortuitous I could select. I wished only for an unimpeded journey. However, the sore spot of this little village was unavoidable. At any rate, you deserve to know the worst and the best, and should be as clear as I am about our situation and hence be in a position to prepare yourself moment by moment to achieve understanding and avoid merely shocking or destructive surprises. So let me warn you that tonight we will encounter only three genuine points of danger, though unhappily the rain has become a kind of general hazard, albeit one out of your hands and of little interest to me. But back to the three genuine points of danger. The final turnoff to the abandoned farm, the Roman aqueduct, and the village we are rapidly approaching —each of these will present us with grave danger, which I will not attempt to conceal, as I have said. However, I am confident about the aqueduct while our journey itself is preparation for the final turnoff which, hopefully, by that time you will encounter as something quite beyond danger. So we may discount the final turnoff. I may even go so far right now as to guarantee you its serenity.

But to be perfectly honest, the village is something else again. It is careening toward us this very moment, only a few words or a few breaths away. Of course the little street through that village is short, hardly more

travesty

than several lengths of the car or one of those sylvan paths that take you from the intersection of two dusty roads to the turnstile at the edge of the field. So it is a short village street but obstinate, and unlighted, and extremely narrow, and bordered for its entire length by a high, sinuous stone wall overtopped by the now wet tile roofs of the village houses and the limbs of an occasional dead tree. Throughout our passage through the wretched place the side of the car will be within touching distance of the heavy stone. If you insist on looking, you will see an infinite rapid shuffling of rock and wood; iron door handles and high broken shutters will fly in your face; our way shall consist of impossible angles, a near collision with the fountain in the central square, a terrible encounter with a low arch. We shall have become a locomotive in a maze, and the noise will be the worst of all. Our lights will be like search-lights swiveling in unimaginable confinement, and a forlorn, artificial rose and the granite foot of one of their crucified Christs and a sudden low chimney will all approach us like a handful of thrown stones. But the noise will be the worst. It will be as if we ourselves were a rocket firing in the caves and catacombs of history. Let us hope that the cats of the village are not as prevalent as the rabbits of our rural highway. Let us hope that we are not deflected by a shard of tile or little rusted iron key or the slick, white femur of some recently slaughtered animal. Otherwise we shall brush the stone walls, swerve, bring down the entire village to a pile of rubble which we shall no doubt drag after us a hundred meters or more.

There is nothing to be done about the sound. But you may well wish to close your eyes, or simply lean forward and bury your face in your hands. The entire deafening passage will last an eternity but also no time at all. Why see it? Why not leave the seeing as well as the driving to me? And you might amuse yourself by considering what the peasants will think when we shake their street and start them shuddering in their poor beds: that we are only an immoral man and his laughing mistress roaring through the rainy night on some devilish and frivolous escapade. Or consider what we shall leave in our wake: only an ominous trembling and a half dozen falling tiles.

But do you see it? . . . Just there? . . . That huddled darkness of habitation? . . . The stones in the rain? . . . Here it is . . . . Hold on . . . .

Come, come, *cher ami*. It is behind us. But now you know how trustworthy I really am.

Do you realize that among all the admiring readers of your slender and now somewhat rare volumes there are those who, if given even the briefest glimpse into your life and mine, would consider me a silly coward and you a worthless soul? If the invisible camera existed, and if it recorded this adventure of ours from beginning to end, and if the reel of film were salvaged and then late one night its images projected onto a tattered white screen in some movie house smelling of disinfectant and damp clothing and containing almost no audience at all, it is then that your malignant admirers would stand in those cold aisles and dismiss me as a silly coward and condemn you as a worthless soul. As if any coward could be silly, or any soul worthless. But then it is what you at least deserve, since you have spent your life sitting among small audiences in your black trousers and open white shirt and with your cigarette in your mouth and your elbows on your knees and your hands clasped—like a man on a toilet—telling those eager or hostile women that the poet is always a betrayer, a murderer, and that the writing of poetry is like a descent into death. But that was talk, mere talk. Now, if given the chance, you would speak from experience.

As for me, I have said it already and will not hesitate to say it again: I am an avowed coward. I am partial to cowards. If I am unable to detect in a stranger some hint of his weakness, some faint gesture of recognition passed back and forth between us furtively and beneath the table, or at least the briefest glimpse of his particular white flag raised in the empty field that is himself, then I am filled with hopelessness, with a sadness as close to despair as rain to hail. But who is not?

travesty

Who in the very depths of the dry well of his "worthless" soul does not loathe the stage setting that holds him prisoner? Who does not fear the inexplicable fact of his existence? Who does not dread the unimaginable condition of not existing? It is easy enough to say that tomorrow you are going to turn into a rose or a flower. But this optimism of the believer in the natural world is the cruelest ruse of all, a sentimentality worthy of children. Of course I am overstating the situation grossly. But if you cannot find the rift in your self-confidence or admit to the pale, white roots of your cowardice where it thrives in your own dry well, then you will never ride the dolphin or behave with the tenderness of the true sensualist.

Only a bumpkin would call your cowardly bad-dreamer "silly."

What, *cher ami*, still arguing? Still unable to put aside self-preservation, the survival instinct, the low-level agitation of the practical mind, the whole pack of useless trumps of the ego? (In the deck that represents the ego all the cards are the same and each one of them is a trump. But these are the liars, the worthless trumps.) But why continue wasting your time and mine by inventing false arguments which I will only refute? Your arguments are hardly gifts to the mind. You are not interested in what they mean. It pains me to see

you pulling them out of your sleeve—another argument, another trump—and in each one to hear you
shout what you have been shouting the whole night:
stop talking, stop the car, set me free. That has been
your only refrain, through all I have said. But why
can't you listen? Tonight of all nights why can't you give
me one moment of genuine response? Without it, as I
have said, our expedition is as wasteful as everything
else.

Let me repeat: you do not want me to take you
seriously but only to heed your shouts in the dark, which
is why for the first time in your life you are not only
wheezing but wheezing on the very brink of savagery.
You are strangling in the ill-concealed savagery of your
resistance. But you know my position. It will not
change. Surely I must be able to strike that one slight
blow that will cause all your oppressive defenses to fall,
to disappear, leaving you free indeed to share equally
in the responsibility I have assumed, short-lived or not.

As it so happens, this particular argument of yours
is just as obvious but perhaps a little more interesting
than the rest, and I have long ago faced it studiously.
Some men, or so goes this line of reasoning, search
with uncanny directness for what they most fear to find.
We rush off to die precisely because death's terrible
contradiction (it will come, we cannot know what it
is; it is totally certain, it is totally uncertain) for some
of us fills each future moment, like tears of poison,
with an anguish finally so great that only the dreaded

experience itself provides relief. We are so consumed by what we wish to avoid that we can no longer avoid it. "Now" becomes better than "later." We run to the ax instead of allowing ourselves to be dragged. And so forth. And as one of the few interesting efforts to make sense of suicide (except for the clinical, to which I do not subscribe) this particular argument of yours has its appeal. We have heard it before, we have listened, it has a good ring. We can imagine the shoe fitting. It is possible, it is exactly the kind of paradoxical behavior that engages all but the bumpkins. And who knows? Perhaps it has cut short the lives of a few bumpkins as well.

But this one is not the lever to pry me from my purpose. My clarity is genuine, not false, while my dread, as you in your pathetic hope imagine it, does not exist. What more can I say? I respect your theory; I respect the fear from which you yourself are suffering (though it oppresses me horribly, horribly); perhaps it would be better for all concerned if just this once I could find you in the right and could hear the shell cracking, so to speak, and all at once find myself overcome with fear and so pull to the side of the road, thus ending our journey, and in rain and darkness sit sobbing over the wheel. Then I could take Chantal's place back there on the floor and slowly, slowly, you could drive the three of us to Tara. In that case you would take to your bed for two days, Chantal would return to her riding lessons, I would follow your lead to the asylum that effected your famous cure.

travesty

So it would go, if you were in the right. But you are not. If I could discover that my clarity is a sham and that I am afraid of death and have devised the entirety of our glassy web because of that same fear of death, I would give myself happily to sobbing over the wheel and spend the rest of my days (after undertaking the cure) in trying to make restitution to you and Chantal. But I can make no such discovery, because there is no such discovery for me to make. Of course I have my qualms. Who would not? But as for this maniacal dread of death that would explain my planning, my determination, my mounting exhilaration as well as my need for a couple of companions, witnesses, supporters to accompany me in the final flash of panic—well, it is unknown to me, your maniacal dread.

But let me be honest. Let me admit that it was precisely the fear of committing a final and irrevocable act that plagued my childhood, my youth, my early manhood, and that drew me with so much conviction and compassion to those grainy, tabloidal, photographic renderings of bodies uniquely fixed, but nonetheless fixed, in their own deaths. And in those years and as a corollary to my preoccupation with the cut string I could not repair, the step I could not retrieve, I was also plagued by what I defined as the fear of no response. It is true. I have nothing to hide. In those days (needless to say I was then no sensualist) I required recognition from girls behind counters, heroes in stone, stray dogs. Let a policeman dip his stick in the wrong direction and I suffered chills in the spine. The frown was my *bête noire*. If the world did not respond to me totally, immediately, in leaf, street sign, the expression of strangers, then I did not exist—or existed only in the misery of youthful loneliness. But to be recognized in any way was to be given your selfhood on a plate and to be loved, loved, which is what I most demanded. But no more. The heat of those feelings is quite gone. I have long since known what it is to be loved. Now, tonight, I want not relief but purity.

But of course I have just now asked you for "one moment of genuine response." So you see how close you have come to the mark.

I do not know why that figure of speech (the kneeling marksman, the drawn bow, the golden arrow) reminds me so insistently of little Pascal. But so it does, the great naked hunter calling forth the little child like a voice from the shadows. Perhaps little Pascal was destined to become a larger-than-lifesize hunter, naked (except for the silver bow, the golden arrow) and stalking his invisible victim among the white boulders beneath a vast sky of unchanging blue. At least I always saw the grown man in little Pascal. By the time he died, when he was not yet three years of age, he had already become a child god, an infant Caesar. Yes, he had already attained his true character by the time he died.

travesty

It is a pity that you had no children. So much intimacy with Chantal surely precludes your thinking of her as your own child. But perhaps it is time for you and me to share Pascal—since anything is possible, and since nothing matters, and since he only exists among the white boulders. But it is true: Pascal has been dead for so many years that he might as well be your son as well as mine. What's that? You long ago decided against fathering children? But everything considered, how right you were. Now that you mention it, the thought of a child surviving you is out of the question. But of course little Pascal survives nothing at all.

And yet who can fail to eulogize our infant Caesar?

He was a fat and contrary tyrant, *cher ami*, and in his third year he began each of our days by subjugating Honorine and me, and even Chantal, to the essential paradox of his fatness, his pink skin, the crown of authority with which he masked his sweet nature. Admittedly, Honorine is not small. But neither is she large in her bones, in her flesh. How then did she mother a child so beautiful in his naked weight, so fatly and gently erotic for all his recalcitrance and pretended ferocity? We shall never know. He was his own source, I often thought, and he is gone. But I saw his little fat body on the spit as often as I saw it crowned; in the chubbiness and gleam of his totally sweet and spoiled nature he was that desirable, that strong.

Yes, he came to Honorine and me with every sunrise, bold and bare, having stripped off his white night-

shirt and wearing only his buttery skin and disapproving
frown and air of infant determination. With every sunrise he pulled away the bedclothes not from me but
from Honorine, who was always his happy match for
nudity. Perhaps you are not able to visualize those morn-
ings. But I see them still: dawn at the window, sunlight
falling across our bed from that window and from the
rose and plum-colored tapestry on our bedroom wall,
the sound of distant bells, the scent of coffee, and the
birds in the air and already the small automobiles congregating somewhere on the cobblestones. And then the
entrance of Pascal, the open door, the light winking
from the long glass handle, and our little naked son
approaching us with his pink cheeks and pouting underlip and little penis which Honorine always used to
touch with the tip of her finger, as if that tiny sexual
organ belonged not to Pascal but to the winged infant
cast in bronze. You must see such a morning as clearly
as I do, *cher ami*, if only to know that in fact I am not
a person who despises life. Quite the contrary.

But in he would come, pouting, wordless, making
his little belly fatter than ever (as might some exotic
fish with air) and in my own arousal from sleep I would
see his bare plumpness and the light in his fine-spun
golden hair. And the lip, the beautiful underlip thrust
out and moist in his unmistakable message: that he
was the joy of all who saw him, but in return there
was nothing in all the world to give him joy. Too ripe,
too beautiful, too lordly, pleasing but never pleased—

such was the fate and character he had created for himself at that early age. But there he would be, the brown eyes filled with accusation, the sunlight flooding the spot where he stood, the tiny spigot crooked and gleaming in the base of the belly. In that moment the faun in the tapestry would quiver at the sight of him and the silver dove on Honorine's commode would fly.

Well, it was always the same. He would wait until I had had my awesome look at him and until Honorine had begun to smile in her feigned sleep and to make her soft welcoming sound, and then cloaked in all his slow assurance he would march across the carpet and reach out one chubby hand and pull the bedclothes from his mother's nude, youthful body. For a moment the two of us, Pascal and I, would gaze on Honorine, who would continue to conceal her wakefulness and, for our sakes, would incline her cheek toward the pillow and arch her back and stretch out an arm and luxuriate in the aroma of her night's perfume.

Do you see her? Do you see Pascal and me? Are you listening?

Well, after that moment, and as if he had received an invisible and all-important sign of acquiescence from Honorine, little Pascal would begin to climb. Yes, with great deliberation he would climb onto our bed (the very same antiquity in which at present Honorine lies sleeping) and then climb onto his mother's warm and well-shaped body. Yes, with frowning difficulty he would mount that body, straddle the hips, seat himself, position himself, until his rosy and sturdy little buttocks were firmly, squarely in place atop Honorine's cluster of purple grapes. There he would sit. Enthroned. And he was quite aware of how he was sitting and how thoroughly his own baby flesh covered and cushioned the flesh of his mother's grapes. I knew what he knew because there was no mistaking the way he would glance in my direction, settle his weight, and then raise his chin in a perfect gesture of self-satisfied defiance.

Then Honorine would open her eyes, she would laugh, she would seize both his hands in hers, with her hips and stomach she would imitate the gait of a trotting horse. Again and again she would murmur *cheri* and beg for a kiss, which he always refused to give her. As for me, at that moment I would wish my little Pascal a good morning, to which inevitably he replied that it was not a good morning but a bad one.

There he would sit holding us in the power of his princely manner and infant eroticism until at last and rubbing her eyes, poor Chantal would appear obediently to haul him away.

How did Honorine survive his death? How did I? But if he had lived, his little body growing and his infant eroticism maturing into impressive masculinity and his head day by day swelling to the round of the laurels, still he would have fared no better than poor Chantal. Actually, he would have fared much worse.

But I myself cloaked his little stone cross in satin. So it is not as if I have never known what it is to grieve.

travesty

But perhaps I am the man little Pascal might have become had he lived. Perhaps it is he who inhabits me now in his death. Who knows?

You will not believe it, but only this morning I visited for the last time my one-legged doctor. Yes, only hours ago and on this of all days, I held up my end of our yearly medical rendezvous. But I am attentive to your every nuance, even to the nuances of your stubborn silence, and now despite your misery and against your will you are objecting to yourself that my concern for my health on the day of my premeditated death (and yours, and Chantal's) is worse, much worse, than rabbits, rain, the invisible motion picture camera with its wet distended lens, the emotional orchestration of the radio you refused to hear. At first glance you would appear to be right: illusory circumstances are beginning to justify your horrified contempt for a man who might be engaged in committing drastic actions not from clarity and calculation but merely to satisfy his inmost urge to saw away on the tremulous violin of his self-love. And yet once again you are wrong. Wrong. Because it was not I who was responsible for this morning's appointment with the crippled physician but rather that elderly woman with the girlish body who is the doctor's nurse and secretary combined. It is true: she notified me of today's appointment long after I myself had figuratively torn today's blank page from my appointment book. And what do you think of the fact that the doctor's rooms are situated directly across from the very restaurant which you yourself happened to choose for your dinner this evening with Chantal, the doctor's rooms and the restaurant facing each other on opposite sides of that same little public garden where the lovers sit holding hands on the cold benches? In other words, this morning while waiting for my medical examination to commence, and stripped to the waist in anticipation of needles and the doctor's archaic X-ray machine, I myself stood at a dusty window in shivering contemplation of the exact same suffering old palm tree which you and Chantal regarded this evening over your soup and wine. But you are already familiar with the pleasure I take in these alignments which to me are the lifeblood of form without meaning.

At the appointed hour, then, I touched the bell button, noting as usual the pathetic opulence of the brass nameplate, and climbed the obviously little-used cold stones to the almost empty room where I inhaled the first trace of that antiseptic smell in which in a few moments I would be engulfed. I heard the air stirring in the rest of his chambers, noted in several chipped, white ceramic ash trays the week-old remains of his dead cigarettes. Of course I was well acquainted with his habit of dragging himself to this very room and seating himself and smoking his cigarettes, reading one of the ancient journals, the doctor waiting alone in the room intended for patients who were never there.

Can you understand the peace and satisfaction I

felt in that place? The visit was perfectly routine, nothing happened out of the ordinary. And yet from entrance to exit I could not have felt more at home amidst all the paradoxes of this establishment: the unused instruments and archaic machines of medical science located within medieval walls; the sound of birds roosting somewhere amongst surgical knives and old books; the faint smell of cooking food which the antiseptic chemical could not disguise; the doctor himself, who was skilled but thought to be unsavory, and who in his own affliction exemplified the general pomposity and backwardness of our nation's corps of butchering physicians and who in his broken marriage exemplified the soundness of our sexual mores. Then too, I knew for a fact that once every week this poor, ruined man sat entirely alone for precisely two hours in a little nearby movie house devoted only to the showing of so-called indecent films. Understandably, it was this habit rather than the missing leg or absent wife that accounted for his unsavory reputation. No wonder I admired and enjoyed his crippled presence.

As I say, there were no surprises. The doctor, as usual, forced himself to walk the length of the corridor to greet me, thrusting to the side one fat, startled hand for balance and swinging in great arcs from the hip his artificial limb, the use of which typically he had never mastered. We met with effusion; he consulted his files; he enquired about my general health and the health of my wife; unbidden I removed my shirt and undershirt; he disappeared; he returned to his desk; the artificial leg obtruded between us in full and menacing view. Again I welcomed silently the trembling hand, the mucus thick in his throat, the cigarette that was burning his fingers. Again I appraised the awkwardness of the ill-fitting leg, noting as usual that our nation is simply not adept at the crafting of artificial limbs because we are not concerned with the needs and imperfections of the individual human body. Again I realized that in the middle of every night the doctor now puffing and coughing beside me, fumbling over my naked chest with his cold and unsteady hands, must lie awake listening to this same artificial leg walking to and fro on the other side of his bedroom door. He was devoting what remained of his life to this hollow leg which wore a green sock and dusty shoe. But dominated or not by the ugly leg, nonetheless he was listening to the strength of my absolutely reliable heart. I regretted that I had never sat beside him in the old movie house.

I waited, I enjoyed the chilly air on the skin of my chest, shoulders, arms; I surveyed the diseased palm tree below in the public garden; I nodded in pleased recognition when the crippled and perspiring doctor knocked one of his full ash trays to the floor, as he always did. I was pleased with the appearance of the nurse-secretary, whose body had the shape of a girl's and the texture of an old crone's. While she drew as usual a handsome quantity of blood from the thick blue vein in my left arm, I listened to the doctor who was breathing wetly through his nose, his mouth, his nose and mouth together. I listened with pleasure; with pleasure I perceived once more that the old nurse-secretary had dabbed herself not with perfume but with the overpowering antiseptic that killed flowers and defined our circumstances.

Time passed like ivory beads on a black thread. My own blood climbed inside the glass. Again I had my brief affair with the old X-ray machine which, after clanking and groaning, rewarded my patience with its sound like a flock of wounded geese in uncertain flight. And I passed exactly the required amount of urine, watched the doctor himself wrapping up the small warm flask with a string and paper, once again marveled that so much painful incongruity could be assembled so awkwardly into a single person.

Well, once again the doctor pronounced me in perfect health, as you would imagine. And of course he suspected nothing, nothing. In all his discomfort and disproportion he retained his purity. Little did he know that in several days and on the other side of the city a laboratory technician, unshaven and smoking a yellow cigarette, would analyze the blood of a man already dead; or that the hazy image of ribs and single lung on the photographic plate would represent only as much reality as the white organs lubricating each other in one of his weekly films.

But there is no justice in the world, since we may safely say that that poor one-legged creature has finally

travesty

lost his only patient, and through no fault of his own. But what, you ask, if even this wretched man continues to live, why shouldn't we? Why does your closest friend not have within himself that cripple's determination to remain alive? Well, let me answer you slowly, quietly. The problem is that you are being emotional again, rather than rational. You must remember that both my legs are sound and that my wife is faithful. Do you understand?

Yes, she is vomiting. But you need not have mentioned it. I have perfect hearing and am just as sensitive as you to those faint, terrible noises. Do you think I am not listening? That I have not been listening? After all, there is nothing worse than painful human sounds unattached to words. And the contents of my own daughter's stomach . . . . Even you will concede that my bitterness would be all the more justified. But I am not bitter. And despite all our so-called natural inclinations, why should we not agree that poor Chantal has earned her vomiting? It is the best she can do. And surely it is no worse than your wheezing.

Actually, the music of melodrama (had you allowed us the pleasures of my superb car radio) would not have been a sodden orchestration of wave upon wave of uninteresting feeling but rather a light, sinuous background of muted jazz. The detached and some-what popular syncopation would have cushioned our every turn while the clear tones of, say, a clarinet would have prevailed and, had he been able to hear them, would have given greater poignancy to the distance be-tween the sleepless goatherd and the momentary, cruel appearance of our headlights in the righthand corner of the wet night. Do you hear that black clarinet? Do you hear the somewhat breezy quality of this dry and sophisticated music? The melody is pleasing, there is even a certain elegance and occasionally a dash of hu-mor in the glassy accompaniment of the invisible piano. How perfect such easy lyricism is for us. What splendid, impersonal sweetness it would have contributed to the tensions of our imaginary and deliberately amateurish film. Well, the radio is already tuned. You have only to extend your arm, reach out with your fingers, touch the knob. But still you are not tempted? Of course you are not. I understand.

A trifle faster? Yes, you are quite right that we are now traveling a breath or two faster than we were. Now is the moment when I must make my ultimate de-mands. As you can see, my arms are stiffening, my fingers are flexing though I never remove my palms from the wheel, my concentrating face is abnormally

travesty

white, and now, like many men destined for the pleasures and perils of high-speed driving, now my mouth is
working in subtle consort with eyes, hands, feet, so that
my silent lips are moving with the car itself, as if I am
now talking as well as driving us to our destination. And
we are approaching it, that final destination of ours. We
are drawing near. Soon we shall be entering the perimeter of Honorine's most puzzling and yet soothing dream.
And now beneath the hood of the car our engine is
glowing as red as an immense ruby. How unfortunate
that to us it is invisible. How unfortunate that the rain
is determined to keep pace with our journey.

But while we are on the subject of invalid doctors
and vomiting children, and since tonight we seem to be
taking our national inventory, so to speak, allow me to
say in passing that generally our physical institutions are
indeed a match for the inadequacies or eccentricities of
our professional personnel. In other words, our build-
ings of public service are as bad as the people who occupy them. Take the hospital nearest La Roche, for instance. I have not had any firsthand experience with
this ominous and in a way amusing place, and in fact
have never seen it. But on good authority and thanks
to my theory of likenesses, which I have already described to you at length, I know for a certainty that
this dark and drafty little place of about twenty beds is

travesty

not equipped with any separate or special entrance for the reception of emergency cases. None at all. A few lights are burning; several cooks are smoking their stubby pipes in the kitchen; the entire drab interior of the place smells like a field of rotting onions. And there is no emergency entrance. No means of swift and ready access between the narrow cobbled street outside and that small whitewashed room to the right and rear where simple first aid may be administered. No access to this small room for bleeding truck driver or possibly his corpse except through the kitchen. The kitchen. It is a scandal. Even our own remains, such as they may be, will be hurried on rattling litters through the steamy kitchen of the miserable hospital near La Roche, that kitchen in which the cauldrons of soup for the coming day will provide a fitting context for the shoeless foot at dawn. Do you see the humor of it, the outrage? But everywhere it is the same: rooms without doors, sinks without drains, conduits that will never be connected to any water supply, corpses or bleeding victims forever passing through the kitchens of our nation's hospitals.

But why, you ask, why this terrible and at the same time humorous correspondence between physical building and human occupant? The answer is obvious: it is simply that there is no difference between the artist, the architect, the workman, the physician, the bloody victim and the cook slicing his cabbage. One and all they share our national psychological heritage. One and all they are driven by the twin engines of ignorance and willful barbarianism. You nod, you also are familiar with these two powerful components of our national character, ignorance and willful barbarianism. Yes, everywhere you turn, and even among the most gifted of us, the most extensively educated, these two brute forces of motivation will eventually emerge. The essential information is always missing; sensitivity is a mere veil to self-concern. We are all secret encouragers of ignorance, at heart we are all willful barbarians.

But indeed, these qualities also account for our charm, our good humor, our handsome physiques, our arrogance, our explosive servility. We are as we wish to be. We would have it no other way. Our national type is desirable as well as inescapable. You and I? You and I are two perfect examples of our national type.

The reason we make such a perfect pair, such an agreeable match, is that you are a full-fledged Leo, while through the marshes of my own stalwart Leo there flows a little dark rivulet of Scorpio. You were unaware of it? But then naturally you could not have suspected anything of my Scorpio influence since I deliberately though casually concealed even the slightest shade of that all-too-suspect influence from your detection. You see how capable I am of deception, at least of any deception which in my judgment is for our mutual good. But thus we have one more scrap to toss on the heap of our triumphant irony. Because in our case it now appears that the poet is the thick-skinned and simple-minded beast of the ego, while contrary to popular opinion, it is your ordinary privileged man who turns out to reveal in the subtlest of ways all those faint sinister qualities of the artistic mind. Yes, you are the creature who roars in the wind while I am the powerful bug on the wall. But you are not interested? You are not amused? And yet if only you would pause a moment to think, *cher ami*, then you would realize that behind my coldest actions and most jocular manner there lies not hostility but the deepest affection. After all, my Scorpio influence inspires me to unimaginable tenderness.

I applaud the dark night. I love the darkness. Not merely for regressive pleasures: for comfort, security, the peace of the dream. No, I am much too active a person to stop with mere sensual immobility, though I am not at all denying my proclivities in that direction as well. No, it is simply that the night is to my eye as is the pair of goggles to the arc-welder. Through the thick green lens of the night I see only the brightest and most frightening light.

For instance, the cemetery we are about to pass— yes, a cemetery, as luck would have it, along with the

travesty

rabbit and gentle syncopation of the muted jazz which,
at this moment, naturally intensifies and quickens—the
cemetery we shall shortly pass is already clear to my
eye, brilliant, rock-hard, motionless. You would see
nothing even if you looked, so don't bother. I see quite
well enough for the two of us. At any rate the cemetery—and now, as a matter of fact, we are abreast of it,
just there on the left—the cemetery stands now before
my eyes, small, rising in tiers, a very old and typically
well-ordered arrangement of crosses and crypts and
mausoleums of black marble, white marble, some kind
of deep gray stone, and it is quite as if we were staring
at that small village of the dead (the likeness is most
appropriate, *cher ami*) from a stationary vehicle parked
in our empty wind-blown, golden field directly across
from that small, excellent example of our morbid ar-
tistry. Yes, that is precisely how totally and clearly I see
our cemetery, thanks to the night. And there is sunlight
but no sun, a quality of deadened daytime colors that
could only be perceived in the blackest and, I might
add, the wettest of nights. The white vases, the red
flowers composed of wax, the sagging ribbons, the tiny
photographs that might have been stripped from an
album depicting all the participants in the last great
war, and the rows of gravel and little barred windows
and stone rectangles constructed to the dimensions of
the human body, and, thank goodness, not a single
mourner to be seen in that entire conglomerate of piety
and bad taste—well, now you have an idea of the true

101

reason I so enjoy driving at night. It is not merely because the roads are generally unused at night. Not at all.

But was that cemetery somewhat familiar to you, *cher ami?* It should have been.

Silence. The bird in flight. Silence falling between driver and passenger who find themselves deadlocked on a lonely road, deadlocked in their purposes, deadlocked between love and hatred, memory and imagination. But you need not bother to raise your chin, turn your head, rouse yourself from all your afflictions into unhappy speech. I know what you are thinking. I could not agree more heartily. Silence is what we are after, you and I. Silence. I long for it also. You are not alone.

We will not be denied. After all, we are now on the near edge of recklessness, it is no longer even a question of time to spare, and beyond us the trees are dying, the tiny shoots are turning a bright green, the landmarks are falling to the left and right of us so quickly that their significance is fading in direct proportion to our mounting preoccupation with ourselves, with what is to come. Yes, silence is consuming sight.

The moral of it all is trust me but do not believe me—ever. Why, even as I deny the fleeting landmarks I cannot help but call your attention to that small church set back from the road in that clump of naked trees on our right. Naturally the church has nothing to do with the cemetery. The cemetery is already far, far behind us. It is gone. No, this is the church that is guarded by the old crone who tends the place with her cane and dog. She is an insufferable old creature who tried to frighten me away the very afternoon I stopped and strolled about and committed the landmark of her ugly little church to memory. She has a beautiful cough, I can tell you that. And I knew at once that she was no more taken in by the weedy sanctity of the little church and mutilated calvary than was I. At any rate I had only an objective interest in the steeple, as a point of essential reference, and a personal interest in the fountain which I knew I would discover in the tall grass behind the church.

The fountain was there, as I knew it would be. And just think, according to local legend it was the Fountain of Clarity. You can imagine how pleased I was to stand in the last of the sun with this precise moment of our dark passage fixed in my mind—hearing the rain, the engine, the tires, seeing our lights—and at the same time to lean forward and regard my own face in the little pool of water that lies in the depths of the Fountain of Clarity. Its ancient artisan could not have known that one day a privileged man such as myself would so admire his work. The creators of that ancient legend could not have known that I have never expected anything at all from my life except clarity. I have pursued clarity as relentlessly as the worshipers pursue their

travesty

Christ. And there I stood, noting the algae in the bottom of the pool, the paleness of the still water, the rough ingenious construction of the fountain hidden in the tall grass. It was a pleasing coincidence. But my own face, our dark night that was as real to me as it is this moment, the automobile that was awaiting me on the dirt road in the shadow of the wretched calvary—it was nothing, nothing at all compared with the intensity with which I was then contemplating the existence of our own Honorine. Your Muse, my clarity, I cannot convey to you my satisfaction as the thought of Honorine filled the silence of an earthly spot which, except for the fountain, was otherwise perhaps a little too picturesque. But if I had ever worn a wedding band, an idea which for me has always been distasteful, certainly I would have removed it then and dropped it as an offering into the cold pool where the cows drank and the old woman filled her jugs and bottles.

No doubt it is just as well that I was not wearing a ring. But tell me, are you feeling better?

Approaching. Yes, we are approaching closer. And once again, you see, I must shift the gears. Shift them from one velvet plateau to the next. And now how directly we are propelled toward Honorine in her mammoth bed. By now she must indeed be smiling in the depths of her sleep. But of course she has left the old lantern burning for us as usual, burning in our honor and for our protection. If I remember, I will point it out to you—that old lantern swaying on the end of its chain.

Jealousy? Jealousy?

After all I have said . . . after my woman of luxury . . . after Monique . . . after all my fervent protestations of affection . . . after all I have done to clarify our situation and to allay your fears—now, as a last resort, you are finally willing to accuse me of mere jealousy? As if I am only one of those florid money-makers who is afraid to thrust even his fingers into the secret places of his stenographer's attractive body and yet turns green, as they say, whenever he imagines that his lonely wife harbors in her heart of hearts the quivering desire to watch while her husband's best friend climbs nude and dripping from his tubful of hot water? Is it with such implications that you expect to stop me, to bring me to earth, so to speak? As if on this note I will suddenly recognize myself and bow to your judgment, exclaiming that, yes, for all these years I have been an excellent actor outwardly while inwardly nursing the most unpleasant banalities of sexual envy? As if you are the hero and I the villain, the one openly and, I might say, foolishly accepting the favors of the other's honest wife and naïve daughter until the other has finally spent enough years drinking slime (in his toilet, in his monastic bed chamber, in his cold automobile parked side by side with his wife's in what was once the stable) in order to act? But are you then so foolish? And could any man, even me, bear such violent feelings for that length of time? And are you suggesting that Honorine is not sensitive, perceptive? After all, if I had in fact been concealing and suffering all this time the latent frenzy of jealousy, would it not have exposed itself in some faint sign which Honorine, in all her concern for my welfare, would have noted at once? Well, you can see what I think of your last resort. This argument is not your avenue of escape.

Of course it is true that you are not a very good poet. I have always made my opinion plain. And it is true that all your disclaimers (about your worth, the size of your audience, the importance of your prizes, the extent of your creative torment, the unhappiness of your life, and so forth) were always to me offensive. And it is true that you are an emotional parasite. Would you deny it? As for your dreadful and eternal seriousness, it is indeed true that on certain occasions, when you have been brooding alone before the fire, when you have been brooding with Honorine over some dull line of verse, when after a glass or two of cognac you have converted your brooding into a sullen, pretentious monologue for the benefit of Honorine and Chantal and me, then I have indeed longed to hear you suddenly give voice to a single, extended, piercing shriek of laughter.

But no more than that. Never have I wished you pain or discomfort more than that. So please do not accuse me of being jealous. It is a bad idea and a poor ploy.

On the other hand, it is also quite true that even after sharing so many intimate years together, still there is a great deal that you do not know about Honorine and Chantal and me. Witness my discussion tonight. And this discussion is, I assure you, the merest hint of what you do not know about the three of us. Only the clear, white, brutal tip of the iceberg, to borrow a familiar but indispensable figure of speech. But wait. Stop for another moment. Consider everything you do indeed know about your mistress and her only two living blood or legal relatives. If you exposed this information in one of your poems you would embarrass the three of us for a lifetime. At least such a revelation would embarrass me if not Chantal and Honorine, who might in fact cherish this permanent form of your devotion.

But have you forgotten it all? Need I remind you of the afternoon and even the hour of day when you wrote your first inscription for Honorine—wrote it, that is, in her copy of your first book of poems? Yes, Honorine's treasured copy of that volume; your earliest and, I later heard, most derivative poems; my own gold-tipped pen which you borrowed for that occasion with hardly a word. Don't you remember? There were times when I might have wished that Honorine had chosen to show me that first inscription of yours, but then there were others when I was equally pleased that she had instead chosen to guard it selfishly from any eyes but hers. At least I caught a glimpse of your black, flowery handwriting that afternoon and, to be honest, thereafter kept my gold-tipped fountain pen capped for a week.

But what of all those first days and months and seasons when I retired early to my own sumptuous but monastic room, took unnecessary business trips, bundled Chantal off to mountain holidays? Have you forgotten how considerate I was, and how discreet, ingenious, flattering? Don't you remember Honorine's pleasure when there were two gifts of flowers on the piano in a single day? Or all those winter evenings when, on the white leather divan, the three of us enjoyed together the portfolio of large, clear photographs depicting the charming pornographic poses of a most intelligent woman of good birth? Surely you remember that visual history of the life of Honorine from youth to middle age in which her own appreciation of her piquant autoeroticism becomes increasingly subtle, increasingly bold? Surely you will not have forgotten the night when you remarked that every man hopes for an ordinary wife who will prove a natural actress in the theater of sex? Well, I savored that remark for days. I still do. It was perhaps the only poetic remark you ever made.

I could go on. I could remind you of our disagreements, which were to be expected, or of our "family" celebrations, such as the event of my fiftieth birthday

travesty

when you decided at last to inscribe one of your precious books for the so-called head of the household. I could remind you of all those physical moments when you managed to convey your awareness of my pleasure, generosity, total absence of perturbation. For instance, I need say no more than "the king drinks!" to recall to you those yearly festive nights when three of us sat around our flower-crowned cake and with shouts of happiness and admiration hailed the fourth. Surely you remember that you were always the king, though I would not remind you of how foolish you looked with your famous cigarette and open white shirt and paper crown. You accepted your royalty begrudgingly, as you did your popularity, but accepted it all the same. Or, for instance, it would be a simple matter for me to say that single word, those several words, which would immediately revive in your memory the sight of your body, of mine, of Honorine removing her nightgown of plum-colored velours before the embers still glowing in the conical recess of her bedroom fireplace.

It so happens that the book you inscribed for me no longer exists. But no matter. You know what I am talking about, and none of it—none of it—can be denied. So you must not accuse me of being jealous. Now is not the time to offer me a wound so deep.

But now I must tell you that once we pass Tara I will say nothing more. And I warn you now that if you

make a single movement or utter a single sound once
we pass Tara your death will not be an ironic triumph
but a prolonged and hapless agony.

And yet I do not mean to adopt that tone of voice.
Will you excuse it? To clear the air, I can tell you that
whenever anything unusual is about to happen my chest
itches. Yes, the skin in the area of my sternum is especially sensitive to unexpected occurrences, changes of
scene, threats of impending violence. And now it is
itching!

Chez Lulu. That's the place. I remember it well.
And how fortunate for me that it is you rather than
Lulu who is my companion for tonight's undertaking,
since Lulu may have been an agreeable and even seductive giant of a young man but was hardly fit for the
mental and emotional rigors of the private apocalypse.
He was an excellent host in the establishment that bore
his name, but I cannot imagine anyone more frustrat-
ing in a discussion such as this one and occurring under
these the most difficult of conditions. Actually our
charming, dark-haired young brute of a man could not
possibly have been your substitute, never fear. And yet
both Honorine and Chantal were fond of him. At any
rate it was in *Chez Lulu* that Chantal gained her emo-

tional though not legal majority in a spectacle that you especially would have enjoyed. Chantal could not have been more than fifteen years of age at the time.

Well, anyone with a penchant for the ocean and for summers promising a certain harmless decadence will recognize *Chez Lulu* from merely its name. You too must have discovered it in a dozen seaside resorts: the harbor barely large enough for a handful of sailboats and a yacht or two, the summer evening rich with the scent of both the rose and the crab, the couples strolling or arousing each other beneath the aromatic trees, and there, fronted by a few feet of powdered sand, there the bar-restaurant which for its disreputable music and growing adolescents and strings of brightly colored lights is indispensable to any such dark and idyllic cove noted for quietude, natural beauty, safe swimming. With *Chez Lulu* the glorious nighttime summer shore would have offered no champagne vying with spilled beer, no irruption of girlish laughter, no hint of first (or possibly last) romance. Perhaps you are already beginning to smile. I need say no more. The point is that until we concluded that we preferred to spend our summers in an Alpine resort instead of beside the sea in the second and smaller dwelling owned by Honorine's mother, Chantal and Honorine and I were among the most favored patrons of *Chez Lulu*. There, I can tell you, we ate mussels roasted on olive twigs and laughed with appreciation at Lulu himself, who as owner and master of ceremonies was large, handsome, amusing,

111

and the possessor of an unlimited store of sexually aggressive ways. You know his type: one of those tall, strapping young men who would have made an excellent athlete had it not been for his relentlessly dissolute nature.

Well, by now you will have the scene in mind: a warm late night at *Chez Lulu*, Honorine and I seated together at a small wicker table at the edge of the sand; the young accordian player and of course Lulu already making spectacles of themselves on a low, crude, wooden stage facing away from the sea and toward the animated crowd of Lulu's favorite patrons old and young; the protective matting of bamboo strips rustling above our heads; the colored lights strung like a bright fringe about the perimeter of the place; the tide going out beyond us in the sultry darkness; Lulu well-launched into the predictable early stages of his exhibitionism . . . . Yes, everything was conducive to what Lulu had promised us would be a night of surprising and superlative entertainment.

Preliminary to this entertainment, a secret event he had been anticipating for us the entire week, Lulu was in the midst of telling one of his rare, evocative stories which always caused Honorine to smile and settle herself more comfortably into her own special attitude of languor and expectation. The story, as we began to discover, concerned a man who had been sent out by his mistress one rainy afternoon to sell a spray of mimosa on one of the town's busiest thoroughfares. The mistress was a beast of domesticity, the rain was heavy, the street was crowded (mainly with children), the man had a face of amazing scars and was so small and stolid that he was not much better than an impressive dwarf. But most important of all, this maltreated and ridiculous figure was the possessor of a left arm nipped off and drawn to a point at the elbow by one of those familiar accidents of birth that are so prevalent in a nation that still lies under the wing of medievalism.

On he talked, our Lulu, now contributing illustrative gestures to his story, which was punctuated occasionally by a few disrespectful notes of the accordian. Well, the stubborn and resentful lover, such as he was, attempted to sell his enormous branch of mimosa in the rain. He held the mimosa first in his right hand and then in a furious grip in the armpit of his offended partial arm, then in an agony of self-consciousness he shifted the mimosa from armpit to angry hand and back again. The children laughed (as did we of Lulu's audience), the hatless man was wet to the skin, a small but elegant automobile drove past with an enormous heap of gleaming, yellow mimosa covering its entire roof. Well, this story had no ending, of course, but afforded the perspiring Lulu a good many artful strokes along with an increasing number of sour notes to the accordianist. And though Lulu wiped his face and laughed and apologized for being unable to reach the moral of his story, no matter how fast and sonorously he talked, still each and every member of his audience smiled in immediate and pleasurable recognition of that moral, which says in effect that we are a nation of persons not only unashamed of the handicapped but capable, as a matter of fact, of making fun of them.

But now came the moment of the rare entertainment that we were all so primed to receive. The laughter faded, Lulu wiped his partially visible bare chest as well as his face with his handkerchief, the accordianist bestowed upon us a great, gleaming sweep of fanfare music, Lulu made a brief but enticing announcement about the spectacle we were now to see. Then he turned and drew aside an ordinary bed sheet which, throughout the story of the unglorious lover, had concealed the rear portion of the small makeshift stage which, I may now assure you, is all that remains of the long-since abandoned *Chez Lulu.*

But that night, and at that moment, already we saw no signs of impending physical decay. To the contrary, because there before us on that little stage stood three young girls who were delightfully natural, only moderately shy, and appealingly dressed in the most casual of clothing—in undershirts designed for boys, that is, and in tight denim pants. The families of those young girls were in the audience, each member of the audience knew each one of those most reputable young girls by sight. Need I mention the clapping that followed the removal of the sheet? Need I say that the smallest and most attractive of the girls was our own Chantal?

travesty

So she was, and barefooted, like the other two, and like them attired to affect simplicity and to erase undesirable differences between the three. As a matter of fact, Honorine and I were pleasantly and simultaneously aware that these three young, innocent girls were already more provocative, more indiscreetly revealed, than most professional seminude girls in a chorus line. You can imagine the activity which this combination (the adolescent amateurs, the public performance) sent rippling through the audience at *Chez Lulu* that night. What, we wondered, had he trained our girls to do? And what were we to make of the three large, orange carrots suspended small end downward approximately a meter apart by lengths of ordinary white twine tied to a slender beam affixed overhead? What "act" could Lulu possibly have in mind?

Well, we had not long to wait. Lulu clapped his hands, the accordianist set aside his great gaudy instrument, we of the audience craned or crowded forward, some of us going so far as to leave our tables and sit informally in the cool sand at the foot of the stage. And then, while the two men bustled about, whispering to the girls and positioning them in an exact giggling line across the impromptu stage, so that each one stood directly behind the particular dangling carrot which had previously been designated as her own, suddenly and as if by prearranged signal, all three girls knelt as one with their faces raised, their knees apart, and their hands behind their upright backs. The tips of the immense

115

travesty

carrots hung barely within reach of the three sets of
pretty lips which, we noticed, had been freshly painted
with a glistening red cosmetic for this debut on the
stage. There were whistles, random volleys of clapping,
more jockeying for better and closer locations from
which to see. But what now, Honorine and I asked each
other with smiles and raised eyebrows, what now—
blindfolds?

Yes, they were indeed blindfolds, and at the first
sight of them, and while Lulu and his grinning assistant were tying them like broad, white bandages over
the eyes of the young trio kneeling as if awaiting the
revolver of some brutal executioner, the audience voiced
its approval and curiosity in a new and sudden spurt
of informality. By now we knew what was coming, of
course, and that we were about to witness some sort
of competition or game which would involve the men,
the girls, and the carrots. We could hardly have been
more aroused or appreciative.

Lulu called for silence, and in the next moment
one could hear even the lapping of water against the
flanks of an invisible sailboat or the sound of insects
in the bamboo matting overhead. All faces were ad-
mirably attentive. We watched as the three girls, now
illuminated in the bright beam of a single spotlight,
shifted nervously in their kneeling positions and gath-
ered their muscles, so to speak, and raised their pretty,
blinded faces like sniffing rabbits. The girls waited, Lulu
raised his thick right arm, the assistant composed him-

self behind two of the girls as might a sprinter. Already the three charming contestants had begun to perspire. Music from a car radio came to us faintly across the little midnight harbor.

Then Lulu shouted, flung down his arm, and thereby sent our trio of sweet girls into an unbelievable flurry of agitation which, we saw immediately, was all the more pronounced and even feverish because of the ground rules by which the girls were forbidden to move their spread knees. In the previous few moments each of us in the audience had made his firm choice, his loyal commitment, and had fixed upon that particular young girl whose efforts he would champion to the very end. And now, even at the mere outset of this simple sport, the shouts of encouragement were deafening.

The rest is obvious, as most stories are. And yet there was indeed a certain mounting excitement, because first it was necessary for each girl to locate her carrot, a process in which all three initially employed merely their good will, their innocence, their straining young bodies (fixed to the rough planks at the knees), the entirety of their groping faces. But as the game wore on, marked by waves of clapping and held breaths, one by one the girls began to intuit what was required of them, began to discover within themselves an abandon which they could not possibly have known until now. That is, they began to grope for the tips of the carrots with their open mouths, with their bright, red, girlish lips now puckered into an oval shape, or at last and skillfully enough began to fish desperately for the fat carrots with their glistening tongues. In all this there was a good deal of tension and comedy, as noses buffeted carrots or a flushed cheek accidentally knocked one of the great orange creatures quite beyond reach. The girls swayed and rose and fell on their spread knees; the carrots swayed in wild circles; the two men became more pressing as pilots, so to speak, of the now hot and sightless girls. Yes, Lulu was devoting all his efforts to Chantal while the accordianist, poor fellow, was obliged to divide his attentions between the other two now frantic girls. Of course it was only too apparent that Lulu and his assistant were attempting to guide their charges toward possession of the unobliging carrots not only with whispered words but with hands that were momentarily visible on a wet and tender shoulder and then, for long periods, were quite invisible in what could only have been their impatient grip on the seat of one of the pairs of tight blue demin pants. The accordianist was not at all in sympathy with his own two awkward girls while Lulu, on the other hand, appeared to be gaining impressive, delicate control over our remarkably responsive Chantal. The black, pointed tip of his shoe was visible between her knees, he crouched behind her like a ventriloquist manipulating an erotic doll.

Well, the admirable young contestants searched in vain, caught the tips of the carrots between eager lips, screamed joyously, thereby once again losing the prize.

travesty

The carrots began to glisten, the denim pants g\~
predictably shaded with perspiration, the girls cried out
in glee or in a childish mockery of frustration. We of
the audience applauded whenever a carrot was successfully trapped, we moaned when that same carrot bobbed
away.

You know the rest: the object of the game, which
was merely the clever excuse for its existence, was to
eat the carrot. And while the two other girls nibbled
and tossed themselves about and even shed pretty tears,
it was Chantal, of course, who finally understood the
game and slowly, sinuously, drew the carrot between
her lips and sucked, chewed, reaching always upward
with her small lovely face, until the deed was quite
beautifully done.

Can you see the hollow cheeks? The tendons in
the youthful neck? The traces of smeared lipstick on the
now devoured carrot? I am sure you can.

Well, Lulu untied the blindfold and, perspiring himself, lifted our happy Chantal to her bare feet to receive
her ovation. And that, of course, is how Chantal became
the Queen of Carrots. It was only the next day that she
found courage enough to go for the first time bare-
breasted to the beach where she spent the morning as
well as the afternoon exerting herself in one of the old,
white, cumbersome paddleboats. Her companion in the
paddleboat was, as you will have guessed, none other
than the notorious Lulu. It was plain to Honorine and
me that Chantal had quite overcome her shyness and

119

that the gigantic Lulu was enjoying to the full this first day with his little pink and amber Queen.

So you think that my brain is sewn with the sutures of your psychosis. So that's what you think. But how very like you to require not a single last resort but two. And if you will remember, I knew it was coming sooner or later, this double-bladed effort first to persuade me of my own psychological distraction, if that is the term, and second to entice me back to sanity, as only you could express the idea, with promises of repose, forgiveness, your imminent departure, the everlasting adoration of my wife and daughter. Of course I understand that you have no alternative but to lay at my door this your actual last resort. As I have said already, it is my opinion that you publicized and glamorized excessively those few months in which you gave yourself over to the sullen immobility of the mental patient. But I am sympathetic. I am well aware that in that short time they so sutured the lobes of your brain with designs of fear and hopelessness that the threads themselves emerged from within your skull to travel in terrible variety down the very flesh of your face, pinching, pulling, and scoring your hardened skin as if they, your attendants, had been engaged not in psychological but surgical disfigurement. I appreciate all this. I regret that you were so abused and that you took such dreadful

pleasure in the line that cracked your eye, cleft your
upper lip, stitched the unwholesome map of your brain
to the mask of your face. But we must remember that
we are talking not about me but you. What I have just
been saying applies to you but not to me. Despite my
theory of likenesses, as I have called it, you are simply
not to think that your former derangement has reap-
peared in me and, at present, is driving all three of us
to what the authorities define as death by unnatural
causes. I believe that if you have been listening you will
have heard in my words the dying breath of your own
irrationality, not mine.

Concentrate, *cher ami*. Concentrate. Because I
know already that I am "adored" by wife and daughter.
It would never occur to me to wish for your "imminent
departure." After all, *cher ami*, it is I who chose you to
be present with me tonight. But on the last point I am
even more confident: you and I would always shun "repose," even if it in fact existed and were not merely
the phantom of all who refuse to present themselves to
the stillness of the open gate.

But now she is dreaming. Yes, if my calculations
are in the least reliable, we are now approximately seven
minutes from Tara where the lady of the dark chateau
lies dreaming. Honorine was always uncomfortable
when, no matter how rarely, I applied to her that ro-

mantic epithet. But of course you are not burdened with her clear integrity and charming modesty, *cher ami*. So tonight I shall indulge myself for the last time and speak of Honorine, my wife, as the lady of the dark chateau. And yet the sleeping rooks; the magnificent shutters drawn closed and only somewhat in need of repair; the stables long ago converted to a garage which, this moment, houses one blue automobile instead of the usual blue car and the beige; the oak tree as bare and formidable as the chateau itself; the stately dog that lies beside the mammoth bed not for protection but for the sake of elegance and love; the amorous grace of the sleeper who earlier dined alone and then at a late hour undressed for bed without fear, without suspicion, and with only a few agreeable thoughts of us. . . . Doesn't all this justify in a way my romantic epithet? The glass of water on the nightstand, the slender volume closed but marked with a ribbon, the sound of breathing, the eyes which, if opened, would be serene —these at least justify my epithet, *cher ami*. But now I must tell you that despite our proximity, despite the fact that we have indeed appeared at the edge of her slumbering consciousness, still Honorine is not dreaming of our approaching car but of a flock of sheep. Let me explain.

One early afternoon, within hours, it seemed to me, of that moment when I conceived of the journey you and Chantal and I were shortly to take—I am being as honest as I possibly can—Honorine and I were walking in one of the distant, rocky fields adjoining Tara. You, I believe, had accompanied Chantal to her riding lesson. The afternoon was fair, the sun was warm, Honorine and I were walking so closely together among the rocks that we brushed shoulders, touched each other hip to hip or hand to hand, pleasantly and unintentionally. A tree far to the west was as small and bright as a golden toy. The rocks were like prehistoric signs to our suede boots. And then Honorine stopped us short and pointed. Because there, just ahead of us, the rocks appeared to be moving while the air was suddenly filled with a music of bells which Honorine, under her breath, described as a kind of heavenly *Glockenspiel*, though in fact she has always been quite as irreligious as her head of the household.

Well, it was a flock of sheep, of course, and we were caught in its midst. Honorine smiled; the tinkling and caroling of the bells increased; a thrush was in flight; for no reason at all the two of us turned and looked back at Tara which, in that soft light was far away and empty and both majestic and shabby, exactly as it had always been and as we wanted it to be. A place of comfort, mystery, privacy, as you surely know. But it was then while the sheep were rippling and purling about our legs (I noted that Honorine was not much interested in the baby lambs, being her typically unsentimental self), it was then and for no reason that I could discern, that Honorine ran her fingers through her short, blonde hair streaked with gray and, keeping a slight distance apart from me, smiled up at my face and began to speak. Without preliminaries and in her clear, quiet way she said that she thought you and I were both a little out of our heads. She said that we were selfish, that we were hurtful, and that she did not trust either one of us. But then she laughed and said that she loved us both, however, and was willing and capable of paying whatever price the gods, in return, might eventually demand of her for loving us both.

You will know how I felt. But may I point out that not once have you raised the question of cruelty or advanced the argument that my insistence on sui-cide and murder—at this juncture let us be honest—may reflect nothing more than my secret desire to punish eternally the lady of the dark chateau, as I may now call her without impunity? Well, allow me to advance precisely that neglected argument of yours and provide an answer as well.

It is cruel. Could anyone know better than I how cruel it is? Yes, what I am doing is cruel, but it is not motivated by cruelty. There is a difference. And who better than I should know that it is in fact motivated by quite the opposite? These are my reasons: first, Honorine is now more "real" to you, to me, than she has ever been; second, when she recovers, at last, she will exercise her mind in order to experience in her own way what we have known; but third and most important, months and years beyond her recovery, Honorine will know with special certainty that just as she was the source of your poems, so too was she the source of my private apocalypse. It was all for her. And such intimate knowledge is worth whatever price the gods may demand, as she herself said. No, *cher ami*, Honorine is a person of great strength. Sooner or later she will understand.

So you see the importance of a woman's dream and a flock of belled sheep.

But I have promised you a glimpse of the formative event of my early manhood. It was nothing, really, though I suppose that in retrospect all of the formative or most highly prized events of our days fade until they no longer have any shape or consequence. At any rate this particular event was the simplest of that entire store which at one time or another defined me, thrilled me, convinced me of the validity of the fiction of living, but which I have now forgotten. I will be brief. A few lines and you will have it.

The automobile, a bright green, was large enough only for two, and I was alone. The street was wide but the hour was such that the crowds, composed mostly of children, were jostling each other from the curbs. I was driving quickly, too quickly, in my desire to visit Honorine, whom I hardly knew. The old man, bewhiskered and wearing a bright silk cravat and carrying a furled umbrella, though the sun was such that it could not possibly have rained that day, was unmistakably one of your kind, which is to say an old poet. From the first instant I saw him he irritated me immensely, hold-

ing by the hand, as he surely was, a child more as-
tounding than any I had ever seen.

I remember the car, which was powerful despite
its size; I remember the street precisely because I was
so uninterested in it; I remember the old poet because
at the very moment I noticed him I saw that he was
gripping the child's hand in lofty possessiveness and
was already staring directly into my eyes with shocking
anger. But most of all I remember the child. She was
a waif with dark hair, dark eyes, an ingenuous little
heart-shaped face filled with uncanny trustfulness and
simple beauty. She was wearing a crudely knitted stock-
ing cap with a tassel and a small once-discarded leather
coat so old that it was scarred with white cracks. I marveled at the child and yet detested the old man who was
already raising his brows, opening his mouth in fury,
drawing back the child as if he could read in my face
the character of a young man who would regard such a
poor and sacred child, as the old man would think of
her, with indifference or even disrespect.

I accelerated. I saw the tassel flying. The old poet's
face was a mass of rage and his umbrella was raised
threateningly above his head. I felt nothing, not so
much as a hair against the fender, exactly as if the child
had been one of tonight's rabbits. I did not turn around
or even glance in the rear-view mirror. I merely accelerated and went my way.

I do not believe I struck that little girl. In retrospect
it does not seem likely. And yet I will never know.

travesty

Perhaps the privileged man is an even greater criminal than the poet. At any rate I shall never forget the face of the child.

What's that? What's that you say? Can I have heard you correctly? *Imagined life is more exhilarating than remembered life* . . . . Is that what you said? *Imagined life is more exhilarating than remembered life.* Can it be true?

But then you agree, you understand, you have submitted after all, Henri! And listen, even your wheezing has died away.

But now I must tell you, Henri, that if you reached your hand inside my jacket pocket nearest to you—an action I would not advise you to attempt despite a moment's gift of agreement—your fingers would discover there a scrap of paper on which, if removed from the pocket and held low to the lights of our dashboard, you would find in my own handwriting these two lines:

> *Somewhere there still must be*
> *Her face not seen, her voice not heard.*

Do you recognize them? They are yours, naturally, and give us the true measure of your poetry. And I may say it now, Henri, I am extremely fond of these two lines. I might even have written them myself.

travesty

But look there. We have passed Tara. And we failed to note the lantern. And now it is gone.

Chantal . . . . Papa has not forgotten you, Chantal!

But now I make you this promise, Henri: there shall be no survivors. None.